QUARTZ CREEK RANCH

AT TOP SPEED

QUARTZ CREEK RANCH

AT TOP SPEED

Kiersi Burkhart and
Amber J. Keyser

SCHOLASTIC INC.

ISBN 978-1-338-28455-3

Text copyright © 2017 by Kiersi Burkhart and Amber J. Keyser. All rights reserved. Published by Scholastic Inc., 557 Broadway, New York, NY 10012, by arrangement with Darby Creek, a division of Lerner Publishing Group, Inc. SCHOLASTIC and associated logos are trademarks and/or registered trademarks of Scholastic Inc.

12 11 10 9 8 7 6 5 4 3 2   18 19 20 21 22 23

Printed in the U.S.A.   40

First Scholastic printing, March 2018

The images in this book are used with the permission of:
© iStockphoto.com/Piotr Krzeslak (wood background).

Front cover: © Barbara O'Brien Photography
Back cover: © iStockphoto.com/ImagineGolf

Main body text set in Bembo Std regular
Typeface provided by Monotype Typography

For every boy and girl who can't believe in themselves . . . I believe in you.

—KB

For my Steamboat family, the real cowboys.

—AK

CHAPTER ONE

Ella glanced once again at the map, then at the upcoming intersection. The green street sign read: BRIDLEMILE RD.

"Dad!" she cried. "You're supposed to turn here!"

Ella's dad yanked the steering wheel to the right, and the car's tires growled over the gravel.

"Could have said something sooner," he said.

"You're driving so fast I didn't even see the turn coming."

"Don't critique my driving. You're eleven."

Ella felt a wave of hot anger, starting in her chest and working its way up her neck. This always happened when they argued. It made all her limbs tense, and her mouth said things she regretted later.

"I get to critique your driving when you get lost and make me two hours late for camp," said Ella as they roared up the gravel road. The car passed under a giant iron archway reading QUARTZ CREEK RANCH, but she barely noticed it—she was glaring at her dad, who sat crouched over the steering wheel, equally furious.

"It wouldn't have been a problem if you hadn't taken so long to get ready at Uncle Nate's house," Dad said as they rolled through the gate, which someone had left open for them.

Ella wanted to throw something. This was supposed to be her trip, but now Dad was ruining it, like he ruined everything when his temper got hold of him. They'd driven out from California and stayed with her uncle in Boulder just so her dad could see the ranch himself, in person, before he left her there for six weeks. He wanted to make sure it was safe and vermin-free, or something like that. Then they'd say good-bye—there were no letters or phone calls allowed until she flew home at the end of camp.

"It's your fault it took me so long to get ready," Ella said as a big ranch-style house sailed by on their right. "You were the one who made me take out and repack my entire suitcase!"

When the driveway appeared, her dad took another sharp turn, jerking Ella against her seatbelt. Then he stomped on the brakes, and when the car had come to an abrupt stop in the parking lot, he ripped the keys out of the ignition.

"I made you repack because you don't even know how to pack your own things properly." Her dad threw open the car door and got out. Ella unsnapped her seatbelt, leaped out, and slammed her door behind her.

"I packed just fine the first time, Dad!"

"You brought way too much stuff." The volume of his voice was steadily rising. "Who needs all that junk at a six-week camp?"

"You don't get it at all!" Ella found herself starting to shout, too, to match him. "Just because I don't wear the exact same thing every day, like you—"

"It's practical, Ell," her dad said, yanking open the trunk of the car. Behind them, the front door of the ranch house opened. A short, wrinkly woman in an oversized T-shirt and curly hair came out first, followed by a pine tree of a man with skin as dark as Ella's, wearing a ten-gallon cowboy hat. A few kids Ella's own age peeked out the door, and another one gazed out the window at them.

"Practical for you," said Ella, starting to sweat in the hot afternoon air as her voice grew louder. "But you can't expect me to wear a suit every day, too! At least what I wear shows I have a personality."

Dad rounded on her. "What do you know? It's about looking professional so I can afford to put a roof over your head and food on the table."

"You go to work every day to pay for all the stupid stuff you buy online!" Each time her dad raised his voice, Ella raised hers more.

"You're such a brat!" shouted her dad, so caught up in the argument that he'd forgotten all about pulling her suitcase out of the trunk.

"And you're a workaholic!" Ella shouted back, starting to spiral with fury. Then she said the thing she knew would really make him mad.

"At least when Mom was around, you came home sometimes."

Her dad's face was turning a dangerous sort of red when the short, leathered woman hopped down the steps and jogged toward them, her expression stunned.

"Hello there," she said, interrupting. "Are you Ella?"

Ella opened her mouth to speak, but her dad glared at her, then at the older woman. "I'm

Jonathan Pierson," he said, then pointed at Ella. "That's my daughter. Ella." He probably thought Ella's skin color had confused the old lady, Ella figured. Since she was half Indonesian from her mother's side, white people sometimes didn't believe Ella was her dad's kid, even though they had the exact same nose and mouth.

"Yes . . ." the woman said, trailing off. "I know." She turned to Ella and smiled. "Welcome to the ranch, Ella. I'm Ma Etty."

Ella smiled back. The old lady wasn't confused—she had just been addressing Ella directly. Ella liked her already. She opened her mouth to respond, but Dad butted in again.

"'Ma Etty'?" he asked, crossing his arms. "Your first name is 'Ma'?"

"It's a nickname."

"Hmm," he said, unimpressed. He gazed around them at the parking lot—the beat-up old pickup, the horse trailers, the tractors. "I was expecting something a little different, for a . . . a rehabilitation camp. So, you're going to work with Ella on her . . . temper issues. Right?"

Ma Etty blanched. "Everyone gets a fresh start here at Quartz Creek Ranch," she said. "We try not to dwell on what brought our kids here, but focus on helping them grow once they've arrived."

"With horseback riding therapy?"

"We don't call it 'therapy,'" she said. "It's just horseback riding."

Dad opened his mouth to say something else, but a low, rumbling voice interrupted them.

"Mr. Pierson," said the ten-gallon-hat man, who had been on the porch a moment ago. He leaned over them. "Let me help you get your daughter's things so she can join us for dinner—get your money's worth, am I right?"

"That's a good point," her dad said, backing away from the car to give the big man access to the trunk.

"This is my husband, Will," said Ma Etty. "Willard Bridle."

"Bridle?" Dad asked. "And that's your real last name, too, I take it."

Ella wished he would just close his mouth and leave already. All the kids had come outside to watch her dad make a spectacle—four kids who looked about Ella's age and two much older teenagers stood on the porch.

Why did her dad have to be so angry all the time?

A month and a half away from him was starting to sound like the best vacation of Ella's life.

"Yes, Bridle is our real last name," said Mr. Bridle. He took Ella's bags out of the car and set them down.

"We'll take it from here, Mr. Pierson," said Ma Etty. "Dinner's almost on the table, and the kids were doing introductions."

"Actually," said a boy on the porch with a blond bowl cut, "we just finished 'em."

For once, Ella's dad looked relieved. Ella was not. She knew first impressions were important—and now she'd made hers by showing up late.

"Great. Thanks, Dad," said Ella.

Her dad wiped his forehead and stood back, not bothering to respond to her jab. He gave Ella a quick hug, and said, "Remember to keep your fists in your pockets. No hitting."

Why did he have to talk to her like she was seven? Ella jammed her hands in her front pockets and pulled away from the hug. Then she took her hands back out again and dropped them by her sides, shooting her dad a spiteful look.

But Dad hadn't noticed, and was already walking back to his car as he said, "I'll leave her in your capable hands, Mr. Bridle, Mrs. Bridle." He opened the door and climbed in. *So much for taking a look around*, Ella thought. "See you in six weeks, Ell," he called out the open window.

Then he peeled out of the driveway with a roar of the engine. The tires kicked up so much dust that everyone in front of the house burst into a coughing fit.

One of the two older teenagers standing on the porch—a girl with long brown hair and a kind face—approached Ella.

"Hey, Ella," she said, extending a hand. "I'm Madison, one of your riding instructors." Ella shook her hand and glanced at the other teenager, a tall black guy now suddenly occupied with breaking up the boy campers, who were prodding and poking one another. He looked like he was probably the other instructor.

"Come on," said Madison, heading past Ella. "Let's drop off your stuff real fast at the girls' bunkhouse, and then we can eat."

\\

As Ella followed Madison across a patchy yard of grass toward two weathered old bunkhouses, she sized up the ranch.

Chickens clucked and croaked in the nearby coop, and the whole place smelled like grass and sky and earth. The faint odor of cow manure reminded her that this place was chock-full of living things.

Impressive. Now that she was here in person, it really lived up to the brochure.

When her dad had laid out all the options for summer "rehab" camp, this feeling was what had endeared Ella to Quartz Creek Ranch—ranch life was supposed to be simple and beautiful, even if a little dirty.

"Remember that camp isn't for fun," he'd said, trying hard to play the role of Dad by using his stern voice. "It's punishment. You're supposed to learn something."

Maybe to him it was punishment, but to Ella, it was a six-week vacation. Horses—check. Ella adored horses. Beautiful, graceful, fast.

And no Dad? Check. She could start fresh here without his oppressive presence weighing her down.

But more importantly, this place was the real deal. The original article. An authentic, working cattle ranch out in Somewhereville, Colorado. Big sky. Gigantic mountains.

Check, Ella thought, looking around. This was

just the place for escaping Petaluma for a while—and the strange, distant way her friends treated her.

After Bianca.

But so what if they were afraid of her now? Nobody should get away with talking to Ella like that—especially about her pigtail braids. Mom had showed Ella how to make them connect in the back like that when she was little. It was hard to do by herself, holding up a hand mirror while she braided so she could see what she was doing, but she'd managed.

So of course Ella popped that trash-talking brat Bianca in the mouth when she insulted Ella's braids. Friend or not, Bianca got what she deserved, as Dad would say. He didn't tolerate insults either.

Madison didn't chatter as she led Ella to the girls' bunkhouse. They ascended a short, creaky set of stairs and ducked inside. The place was clearly built to house more than just two girls—there was room for at least five, probably more if the table were scooted aside for another cot. Ella wondered if, by chance, the Bridles ever ended up with all girls and zero boys.

That would be a big mess, Ella thought.

Top bunks were always the most fun, so Ella headed for the one nearest the window. "I've got to grab something," said Madison, pointing to the door of a separate room. "Just so you know, I sleep in there. Bathroom's over there." She gestured to the next door over. "Drop your stuff on whichever bunk you want, and let's head back."

"Aye, aye, cap'n," said Ella. She walked down the short row of bunks and stopped at the middle one, by the window. Perfect. The light came in just right so if she slept on the top bunk, she'd feel it on her face as the sun came up.

If there was one silly phrase her dad always said that Ella actually took to heart, it was, *Early to bed, early to rise, makes a man happy, healthy, wealthy, and wise.* He said it often, with emphasis on the "wealthy" part.

While Ella didn't really believe in the proverb, the early morning was quiet and calm—if she could get up for it. Having the morning light pour in on her face would help immensely, she thought.

Yes. This bunk would do great.

But when she got up to the top of the ladder and set her suitcase down on the bed, she found another girl's duffel bag already sitting at the foot.

Ella picked up the duffel. This girl, whoever she was, would just have to be happy with the other top bunk by the door. Ella tossed the ratty duffel over to the next bunk, then set her own by the pillow and dropped back down the ladder.

She met Madison at the door.

"Burgers," was all the trainer said, and they headed back to the ranch house.

CHAPTER TWO

When Ella and Madison walked inside, everyone was already sitting at the table in the dining room, assembling hamburgers. Paintings of galloping horses hung everywhere, and the house felt welcoming and rustic.

Ella took the one open seat left, between a brown-haired girl and a tall, wiry boy. The girl didn't even look up as Ella sat down. She was too busy eating. The boy, who looked vaguely mixed-race—probably the way she looked to others, Ella thought—turned toward her instantly.

"Hey!" he said, his mouth full of food. Ella leaned away a little as he kept talking, faster than she could keep up. "Bummer you got here late! We had homemade churros earlier, before dinner. It was great. I mean, dessert before dinner? Who gets to do that?"

"Yeah," Ella said, ignoring him as she forked the last hamburger onto her plate. She asked for the buns, which had to get passed from the opposite end of the table.

"Everyone," said Ma Etty from the head of the table, "let's do another round of introductions real quick for our newcomer, okay?"

"Aw," said the short kid with the awful blond bowl cut. "You can't recapture improvised genius or it just feels recycled. My bit about hamsters and basketball wouldn't be the same." He spoke with a thick Texan accent.

The tall boy next to Ella laughed. "How would they be able to hold it with those tiny, tiny hands?"

Great. They already had inside jokes. By being late, Ella was even farther outside the circle than she'd thought.

"Awright now," said Mr. Bridle. "Let's tell Ella your name and where you're from. I'll start." He cleared his throat. "I'm Will Bridle, and I live on this ranch with my lovely wife, Henrietta." He leaned over and kissed her cheek. One of the boys

14

covered his face so he wouldn't have to watch.

Madison waved to Ella. "We already met," she said. "I'm Madison, I'm a trainer here, and I'm gearing up for tryouts again for my college swim team."

The teenaged guy next to her just dipped his head. "Fletch," he said. "Horse trainer, bronc rider, human being. Nice to meet you." Then he nodded to the Texan next to him, who sat across from Ella.

"I'm Ash," he said around a mouthful of hamburger, then swallowed it down with orange juice. "Ash Feezle. I'm from Dallas, home of the Cowboys. America's Team." He tapped the logo on the front of his Cowboys T-shirt. "Kind of ironic, now that I think about it . . . Sent away for the summer to become a real cowboy."

Introductions moved around the table to the boy sitting next to Ella.

"I'm Drew," he said, smoothing back some of his curly, dense hair. It was cut tall on top of his head and shaped kind of like a boat. "Drew King. Not like Martin Luther King. Everybody asks that because my mom's black, but you know, that's a stereotype of black people to just assume I'm related to MLK because my last name is King."

Ella had not assumed that, but she nodded anyway. Motor-mouth went on.

"And I think everyone assumes that stuff about MLK because I'm from Atlanta, but it's a great city. Everyone should make a point of visiting Atlanta, especially during peach season. We have every variety. Except maybe don't come next year, because I accidentally rode my BMX bike through all those experimental saplings and kinda ruined them—"

"That's plenty," said Ma Etty, interrupting him. "Thank you, Drew. Now, Ella? Will you tell us a little about yourself?"

Ella had thought about this on the drive up, so she was prepared.

"My name is Ella Pierson," she said smoothly. "I'm going into sixth grade at my new school in Petaluma, California. My favorite activities are drawing, riding my bike, and hanging out with friends. I'm excited to be here and meet everyone." She glanced around the table, smiling at each of the other kids in turn. They looked back at her like she'd descended from a UFO.

Ma Etty blinked. "We're glad you could make it, too, Ella."

Ella nodded back gracefully. If the other kids wanted to act like they'd been sentenced to six weeks in prison, that was their problem. She was excited about this place, even if they weren't.

Introductions continued with the girl sitting next to Ella, who so far had not spoken. Now, Ella had a chance to size her up. She looked almost like a young version of Madison: hazel-brown eyes, with long brown hair tied back in a ponytail and a pretty face.

"I'm Jordan McAdam." The girl didn't even look at Ella. "I'm from California, too, actually. Pretty close to you. Near Clearlake."

Ella hadn't been near Clearlake much. *Only red-necks live out there*, Dad would say. But it explained something about how Jordan was dressed. Ella might not have noticed her clothes except in comparison to Drew, who sported a fresh, striped T-shirt from American Eagle and new-looking dark jeans. Jordan wore a thin flannel shirt that looked a century old and a pair of holey, stained jeans.

"Clearlake," said Ella, trying to think of something nice to say. "Not much out there."

Jordan shrugged and went back to her dinner.

Ma Etty coughed.

"Okay, thank you, Jordan. Next?"

It was the last boy's turn. He sullenly looked up from eating.

"My name is Kim," he said. "Kim Do Yung. I'm from New Hampshire. I traveled an exceptionally long way just to get dirty and clean stalls." He made a face. "My dad teaches Korean at Dartmouth College, and my mom teaches Communications."

Both Drew and Ash chuckled.

Kim glanced at each of them. "What?"

"Nothing," said Ash, laughing harder. "It's just . . . is your name short for Kimberly?"

Kim gave him a flat look. "No. It's Korean. And in Korea, Kim is a boy's name."

Ella saw her chance to redeem herself in front of the Bridles after her dad's fit in the parking lot—but Jordan spoke first.

"Some names are both," she said, still not looking up from her food. "Like mine. I've met tons of boy Jordans, and a few girl Jordans, and that's just in California."

"It's a great point," said Ma Etty. "A lot of names can go either way. And around the country—sometimes you'll meet people with names that seem strange to you. Your name, Drew, is probably strange to a lot of people."

"Uh . . ." He looked momentarily perplexed. "Because it's not a nickname for Andrew, like most people named Drew?"

"Exactly."

Ash rolled his eyes. "Not really that strange," he muttered.

"I like it," said Ella, not wanting to miss her chance to chime in. "Kim is a nice name for a boy."

But Kim glared at her. "My name isn't 'nice,'" he said. "It's fierce."

Ella returned the look and bristled. She'd just been trying to help.

"Ooh," said Ash. "*Fearsome* Kim. He's short. He's scary. He'll suffocate you with kimchee."

In an ESPN voice, Drew said, "Our next wrestler is Fe-e-e-earsome Kim!"

Kim looked like he wouldn't mind putting his fork through Drew's eye.

"All right, all right," said Ma Etty, holding up both hands. "No making fun of anyone at my dinner table."

"We weren't making fun," said Ash. "We were imagining Kim's pro wrestling secret identity."

Ma Etty exhaled sharply. "None of that, either."

"Who ate all the hamburgers?" asked Drew, picking up the empty plate. Ella wondered if this guy would ever shut up.

"New girl did," said Kim, pointing at Ella as she took a bite of her hamburger.

"But I'm still hungry!" moaned Drew.

"Right," said Ella, trying her hardest not to get mad. "Sorry for taking one whole hamburger so I don't starve."

"Can't let her starve," said Ash.

"But what about me?" said Drew. "What if I starve?"

Ella started steaming. What was wrong with these kids? And was she really stuck with them for the next six weeks?

"Have more potatoes instead," said Fletch, passing the bowl of home fries.

"Potatoes do not equal meat," said Ash, and the table devolved into another argument.

Under her breath, Jordan said, "I guess introductions are over."

Ella took a big bite of her hamburger to occupy her hands. She was already hankering to sock one of these idiots right in the mouth, but she stopped herself. She couldn't mess this up already—not after promising herself a fresh start, away from Dad and his temper.

It was going to be a long summer.

\\\

Even though it was dark, finding the way back to the girls' bunkhouse was easy with the boys galloping ahead of them across the chicken yard.

"Fe-e-e-earsome Kim!" Drew shouted, sending the chickens squawking back to their coop.

"Shut up, dude!" hissed Ash.

"Don't boss me around, Dallas."

"I'm going to put earwigs in both your ears if you don't be quiet," said Kim. "While you're sleeping."

Fletch had tried for a little while to corral them into some semblance of order, but it looked like he'd already given up as the boys ran up the stairs of their bunkhouse and vanished inside, hooting and hollering and sulking respectively.

The girls' bunk was stone silent in comparison. Madison went into her room to start getting ready for bed. As Ella took off her shoes at the door, Jordan climbed up the ladder to the bunk near the window.

"Oh," she said. "My duffel bag is gone."

Here come the water works, Ella thought.

Madison peered out of her room. "Your bag is gone?" she asked, eyebrows drawing together. "I hope one of the boys didn't come in here and swipe it, thinking they'd play a practical joke."

"It wasn't the boys," Ella said, neatly stashing her new white and pink sneakers next to Jordan's scuffed, dirty ones. "I moved it. I wanted that bunk for the light to help me wake up in the morning, or else I'm all groggy and grouchy. And you don't want to see me grouchy in the morning."

A frown crossed Madison's face. "Ella, it's first-come, first-served," she said. "And Jordan called that bunk first—"

"It's fine," said Jordan, hopping back down the ladder, then going up the one nearest the door. There, she found her duffel bag waiting and nodded to herself. "I don't care which bunk I have."

"Are you sure?" asked Madison, still watching Ella, though she was speaking to Jordan. "Because—"

"Really. It's fine, if she likes that one."

Ella knew fake when she heard it, and it didn't sound like Jordan was putting it on. She seemed unperturbed.

Madison's eyes narrowed.

"I'll sleep here just as well as there," Jordan said again. With that, she climbed up onto her bunk and started digging through her duffel bag for her toiletries, like nothing had happened.

Shrugging, Madison ducked back into her room, but not before shooting Ella a meaningful look. But Jordan obviously didn't care, so why should Madison?

By bedtime, Jordan still hadn't said another word. Madison suggested they give their cabin a fun, cheery name before bed, a camp custom. Ella thought it was lame, but after the duffel bag incident, she wanted to get back in Madison's good graces.

"What about—the Cowgirl Cabin?" said Ella. She imagined herself in a big Western saddle with a rope hanging from the horn, dressed in her best chaps.

Madison turned to Jordan for her opinion. Jordan just shrugged.

"Is that a yes?" Ella said impatiently.

"Sure," said Jordan.

"Cowgirl Cabin it is," said Madison. But *sure* was a pretty lackluster recommendation, and it annoyed Ella that she'd had to pick the name alone.

When Madison said good night and closed her door, she promised tomorrow would be a day of meeting horses and learning their way around the ranch. Ella couldn't wait.

As the lights clicked off, Ella lay in bed expectantly, waiting for Jordan to say something in the dark. Ella loved to talk after the lights went out at sleepovers, when you could no longer see one another's faces, but could still make out voices whispering, just out of the adults' earshot.

Except that Jordan said nothing. At some point, her breathing evened out, and Ella realized she'd gone to sleep.

She didn't quite know what to make of Jordan. Tomorrow would be interesting for more reasons than just horses.

CHAPTER THREE

Ella woke to warm sunshine drifting across her eyes. She opened them, rubbing the sleep from their corners, and let out a creaky yawn.

This was just how she wanted it. Dinner last night hadn't gone perfectly, but today would. She was Ella Pierson: thick, silky black hair like her mom's; a small, round face; and big dark eyes that could melt the hearts of most adults. And she was going to ace this horseback riding thing, like she had aced drawing, and math, and bicycling. That's what Dad had said.

It was early, so Madison's door still sat closed. Sitting up in bed, Ella expected to look over and see Jordan passed out on the next bunk.

But her bed was empty, the blankets strewn around. Strange. Ella shook her head and crawled down her ladder.

Going to put on her sneakers, she found Jordan's dirty ones were already missing. Where had she gone this early in the morning?

As she laced up her shoes, Ella spotted a new addition to the shoe rack: a small pair of worn riding boots, so dirty and well-used she couldn't tell if they'd originally been brown or black.

Ella's boots still sat, brand-new in their box, in her suitcase. She'd kept the box so the boots wouldn't get her clothes all dirty when she flew home, and had to repack twice to make it fit.

But Jordan had riding boots already—ones that looked thoroughly broken in. Ella wondered if Jordan had ridden horses before.

Couldn't be. This place was for kids who wanted to learn how to ride, not for kids who already did. That had been Ella's impression after reading the brochure that said, verbatim: *Learn to ride at Quartz Creek Ranch*.

When she chose horse camp, Ella had done it knowing she was going to be a natural on horseback. Today was the first day of lessons—her day to shine.

So why had Jordan come here, if she already knew how to ride?

\\\

Jordan returned just as Madison started shuffling around in her room, and she mumbled something to Ella about taking a walk. When Madison stumbled out into the main room, she found both of her charges already awake, washed, dressed, and ready for the day.

Ella didn't ask Jordan about where she'd gone that morning, and Jordan didn't offer an explanation. Like last night, she stayed silent through breakfast, focusing on her eggs, bacon, and toast like it was the highlight of her Saturday morning.

But it wasn't even nine in the morning and the boys were already arguing. Drew claimed that Kim had spit on his toothbrush so he wasn't going to use it, and Ash—horrified and disbelieving that someone would refuse to brush his teeth for the next six weeks—begged Kim to intervene on behalf of everyone who would have to smell Drew's breath. Kim just glared at both of them and said, "If I was going to mess with someone's toothbrush, merely spitting on it would be at the bottom of my list of nefarious toothbrush deeds."

And then Ash didn't know what "nefarious" meant, and he accused Kim of intentionally talking in a way that he couldn't understand to hide his guilt. In the meantime, Fletch looked like his spirit had left his body and gone on a peaceful, astral hike.

"So what if he spat on your toothbrush?" Ella finally asked, working to stay calm. Their nonstop arguing grated her nerves. "Just wash it off."

"It's not like a hair brush," Drew said, rising into falsetto on the last words. "It goes on your teeth. In your mouth."

"So?" said Ella. Her voice rose. "You know what else goes in your mouth? Forks. And forks get washed and reused every day. That fork in your hand was probably in three different mouths yesterday."

Recoiling, Drew said, "Gross!" and dropped his fork. Ella rolled her eyes. Maybe the fact she'd shown up to camp late didn't matter. These kids were completely lost in their own stupid world.

Maybe she understood why Jordan stayed silent and out of the way.

\\\

The day was already hot, so the air inside the dark horse barn hit Ella like a splash of cool water. She stood among the rows of stalls, listening to horses snorting and eating inside. It renewed Ella's faith that this camp had been the right choice. Even Drew, who had come to the barn with Fletch, went silent as they stepped inside the cool quiet, and the heavy wood door closed firmly behind them.

As Ma Etty had outlined for them at breakfast, the trainers had hand-picked a horse for each of their students based on the short questionnaire they'd filled out. Behind one of these stall doors was a horse chosen just for Ella—a horse that she, and only she, would ride for the next six weeks.

"Ella?" Ella glanced up as Madison said her name. "Come with me. It's time to meet Figure Eight."

Figure Eight? Ella's heart leapt. What a fantastic name for a horse—for *her* horse.

Madison led her to the very end of the hall, where the last stall on the left had a gold plate on it that read *FIGURE EIGHT.*

Peering into the stall, Ella was surprised to find, well . . . nothing. No horse—just some scattered hay and manure. She turned around to ask Madison where the horse had gone and saw the trainer holding out a treat through the bars of the stall. There was a sudden, loud thump inside.

Knobby knees rose up from the floor. The horse had been lying down against the wall, making itself partially invisible. Now it straightened its front legs, stretching as it got up, and lapped the treat out of Madison's hand before it was even standing up straight.

"Figure Eight's kind of a weirdo," said Madison, as Figure Eight walked into the light. "She likes to rest lying down."

Figure Eight was also gorgeous—mostly white, but splattered with big splotches of light doe-brown, like an abstract painting. The brown covered both of her eyes, and the spots made her mane different colors as it ran down her neck. Ella knew right away Figure Eight was the perfect horse. You could see it in her lean, muscular body; in her graceful movements as she got to her feet; and in the shape of her square, strong head.

"Ella," said Madison, "please meet Figure Eight. She's one of Ma Etty's favorite horses—very beloved by everyone at QCR."

"I can see why," said Ella, as Figure Eight's soft, curious white nose pressed between the bars.

"We call her Eight for short," Madison said, taking a halter off the hook. She showed Ella how to safely open the stall door, step inside, and put on the halter. Once Ella got Figure Eight out of the stall, she could see all of her.

Yes, Ella would look fantastic riding Figure Eight.

Madison walked Ella through the process of brushing her coat, then picking the tiny stones and caked-in manure out of Eight's strong hooves. When they were done, Figure Eight simply gleamed. Ella's pulse thrummed with anticipation.

Madison led Ella and Eight to the arena out behind the barn, where Drew was leading his own horse—a light brown gelding with stocky legs and a blaze down his face—around the perimeter. There, Fletch was waiting, and he gave Ella basic handling instructions.

"Walk around the arena; get used to each other. Keep Eight walking next to you with her head at your shoulder, listening to your movements. She should respect your personal space and not get distracted eating grass."

Madison left to get Jordan, leaving Ella and Drew with Fletch as they led their horses around the arena.

Drew talked nonstop while they walked, but Ella

wasn't listening. She was thinking about Jordan's worn, dirty riding boots.

Drew persisted, and Ella had started to grow annoyed when suddenly the barn door opened and Jordan emerged. She led a big, tan buckskin horse with charcoal-gray feet, mane, and tail. That hadn't taken long, Ella thought.

"Where's Madison?" asked Ella as Jordan took up leading her horse behind Ella and Drew.

"She sent me into the barn to get Loco Roco," Jordan said, gesturing to the buckskin horse, "but then had to go get Ma Etty's help with Ash and Kim. They were having some . . . difficulties."

Madison seemed to trust Jordan a lot. Ella's heart beat more quickly.

Soon the other kids joined them, and the lesson started. Fletch and Madison walked them through basic handling procedures: turning, stopping, backing up. Eight executed each task with precision and, it seemed to Ella, a bit of boredom. This baby stuff was below Figure Eight.

Good. They were the perfect match she'd imagined.

Ella wanted to get on to the riding part, but the handling wasn't so easy for Kim, Ash, and Drew.

"You're messing up my mojo," Ash told Drew, huffing as his horse once again resisted backing up. "You're too close."

"Maybe you're the one who's too close, Dallas," Drew shot back. Hooting with exhilaration, he said, "I'll show you how this backing up thing is done!" and flung his lead rope around, trying to get his horse to take a step back.

But Drew swung the rope too hard, making a wide, threatening arc. The horse threw his head up, afraid of getting hit by the blunt end of the rope, and jerked away. He bumped into Jordan's horse, surprising him. Loco Roco instinctively threw his ears back and shot out a warning kick. The kick barely missed Drew's horse, but it left a dent in the arena fence.

"Drew!" said Fletch, jogging over to take the lead rope from him. "I said swing it lightly—not try to lasso him."

"She was in my way," said Drew, pointing at Jordan, who had been minding her own business. Jordan said nothing, but put more space between Loco Roco and Drew's brown bay horse. He was such a jerk, Ella thought.

"Regardless of where everyone else is, it's your

job to keep an eye on yourself and your horse," said Fletch. "But I don't think that's the problem here. Remember, horses are flight animals. They need a calm, collected rider to be constant and trustworthy, not shouting and flailing around. That will only frighten him and make him want to run away from you."

"I wasn't flailing," said Drew.

"You were totally flailing," said Kim with a laugh. Ella wanted both of them to shut up so they could get back to the lesson.

Fletch turned. "Thank you for the input, Kim, but it's unnecessary."

"Whatever," said Kim. He tried to get his own horse to back up, obviously trying to show off, but his motions were erratic, and the horse flattened his ears and stamped. When Kim saw he was only humiliating himself, he grew annoyed and swung the lead rope faster.

"Controlled, confident motions," called Fletch. "You don't need to make yourself louder for your horse to hear you."

"I wasn't saying anything," said Kim, scowling.

"But you were," said Fletch. "When you fling your lead rope around like that, it's like you're yelling at your horse, 'Back up!' But you don't need to yell. You can whisper, and he will still hear you. He's listening." Fletch took the lead rope and, gazing directly at Kim's horse with a gentle, patient look on his face, he said, "Back."

He only had to give a tiny flick of the lead rope for the horse to take one polite step back. How was Fletch so patient? Ella would have screamed at Kim by now. She already wanted to knock him flat on his back.

Kim snatched the lead rope back. "I can do that." He tried to mimic what Fletch had done, but his energy was anything but gentle and patient. Instead of backing up as Kim threw the lead rope around, the horse let out a nervous whinny and tossed his head. Kim snarled, "What's wrong with you, horse?" He flung the lead rope on the ground and crossed his arms. "I shouldn't be sentenced to this just for cussing a little on paper. Horses suck!"

Ella turned to Jordan.

"I don't think your horse is the one who's loco around here," she said, as Fletch retrieved the lead rope and tried to talk Kim down.

But Jordan just shrugged.

So much for girl kinship.

CHAPTER FOUR

They didn't get to ride at all their first day of lessons, which Ella felt was gravely unfair for a place calling itself a riding camp.

At lunch, Ash started to tease Kim about his outburst in the arena. "So you got sent away to camp for writing cuss words?" asked Ash. Kim gave him the stink-eye.

"It was a letter."

"To who?"

"Some girl. She dumped me."

"Hoo!" said Ash, slapping his thigh. "You wrote a girl a mean letter because she dumped you?"

Kim looked like he was about to snap back when Fletch let out a weary sigh. "Let it go, Dallas." In his impatience, Fletch had even adopted Drew's silly nickname. "You'll all have another chance at horses again tomorrow."

"And you'll get to ride then, too," Madison said brightly.

"Why didn't we ride today?" said Ella. "All that stuff we did seemed pretty useless. I want my money back." But she smiled.

Ash and Kim chuckled at her joke.

"Learning proper handling is anything but useless," said Mr. Bridle gruffly from the other end of the table. "You need to be able to completely control your animal, even when you're not riding. You won't always be on a horse's back. How can you get on a horse you don't even have a relationship with yet, and expect him to trust you?"

Ella fell silent. No one at the table had a smart-aleck response for Mr. Bridle.

After lunch, Fletch and Madison handed out chores. Ella ended up walking the whole pasture fence with Ash, checking for breaks and weaknesses. He talked incessantly about football and his beloved Cowboys.

"I already told you that I have zero interest in talking about football," Ella said, turning on him. "So shut it, Dallas!"

After that he sulked, which was fine with Ella, because it meant he was quiet.

But by afternoon free time, all that walking had made her calves ache. Dinner was a mess of food and noise as the boys argued about football teams, whose horse was cooler, and the proper amount of condiments to go on the Polish sausages that Ma Etty had served. It escalated to shouting, until Ma Etty let out a loud whistle.

Everyone stopped talking.

"I know it was a big day," she said, "but around the dinner table, I expect better. If you have a lot of leftover energy, there's always more work to do around the ranch that I can assign to you during your free time tomorrow."

The kids around the table stayed quiet. At this rate, the three boys would lose all their privileges, probably for the rest of camp.

Ella couldn't believe she was stuck with these people for the next month and a half.

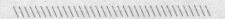

When Ella got up the next morning, Jordan was gone again.

Putting on her sneakers as quietly as she could to avoid waking Madison, Ella slipped out of the bunkhouse into the cool morning air. Sunrise hadn't been that long ago. What was Jordan getting up to do at dawn every morning?

After half an hour scouring the ranch, birds singing their morning songs in the rustling trees, Ella still hadn't found Jordan. It was almost time for breakfast. In a last effort, Ella went inside the barn and wondered why she hadn't checked here first.

Loco Roco's stall door stood slightly ajar, just enough for a slender girl to slip through. Inside the dark stall Jordan stood by Loco's side, stroking his neck as he ate some hay.

Ella felt like an intruder in the cool morning silence. She kept out of sight, and it didn't appear that Jordan had heard her come in. The quiet girl was engrossed in her own thoughts, sliding her hand from Loco Roco's forehead down to his wither, ruffling his mane as he worked through his meal.

Backing away, Ella treaded silently out the way she'd come in, not feeling any more enlightened about the mystery that was Jordan McAdam.

\\\

Even breakfast couldn't be a peaceful affair. Kim refused to eat his waffles on the notion that the holes made them inedible (though pancakes were apparently acceptable), and when Ma Etty suggested he fill the gap in his stomach with more sausages and fruit instead, Ash pinched the bridge of his nose.

"Kim was already farting all night," he said, "and now you're giving him fruit? Do you hate us?"

"That was Drew," said Kim, not even looking up from his plate.

"Nice try!" Drew barked out a laugh. "Passing the blame on to me—really, a solid attempt."

"Oh my god." Ella set her fork down on the table with a resounding noise. "Do you guys ever stop? Ever?"

"Someone got up on the wrong side of the bed," said Ash. He was probably still bitter at how she had shut him down yesterday.

"I got up on the perfectly right side of the bed until I came in here and had to be around you idiots!"

"No one at my table is an idiot," Ma Etty said. "And I don't appreciate name-calling." Ma Etty was chastising her, not them?

"It's not name-calling when it's true," Ella snapped, getting to her feet. The burning thing under her skin grew hotter. "I'm just defending myself!"

"Okay, okay," said Fletch, raising his hands. "Ella, sit back down and finish your breakfast." He turned to the boys. "What you said to Ella was pretty rude, too."

"She told me to shut up yesterday," said Ash. Ella clenched her hands under the table.

"Doesn't matter," said Fletch, and even his endless patience seemed to be running thin. "Eat. Then we're going to go ride some horses."

\\\

But breakfast couldn't ruin the excitement Ella felt as she found Figure Eight in her stall again, all fifteen hands of muscle and beauty just waiting to carry Ella off into the sunset.

She remembered Jordan in that stall with Loco Roco this morning, silently stroking his powerful neck. They'd looked so peaceful, so lost in their own shared universe. Ella paused long enough to give Eight a few pats of greeting before putting on the halter and leading her out of her stall.

"Eight is such a pretty paint horse," Jordan said, approaching with Loco Roco.

"Yeah," said Ella, nodding vaguely. "A pretty paint horse, all right." She didn't know what a paint horse was, of course, but she had an idea there was one standing right in front of her, covered in brown splatters.

Out in the arena, Madison did a small demonstration on saddling and bridling with her horse, Snow White, a beautiful little white Appaloosa with black spots all over her rear end. Then the kids saddled their own horses, and it was time to ride.

Fletch walked them through the basics—getting the horses walking, good saddle posture, neck reining. "Pull the reins in the direction you want to go," Fletch instructed. "Right across the neck." Ella didn't understand how this could tell a horse where to go, but it seemed to work if she tugged hard enough.

Remarkably, everyone appeared to be on good behavior. Ella was grateful; she didn't want any distractions keeping her from paying attention and cataloguing all the advice Fletch gave them so she could master this riding thing as fast as possible.

"Okay," said Madison, raising a hand for attention. "I want everyone to start into a walk. Keep your horses along the rail—that means, as close to the fence as possible. Don't let them cut corners."

The first few laps around the arena, Figure Eight kept close to the rail, staying at an even walk. Ella let the reins hang loose, as Fletch had instructed.

This was a breeze. Elation raced through Ella's nerves. She could do this, no problem! Eight's even, smooth gait felt like a dream.

On the third lap, Madison called out to them. "When you reach the far end of the arena—see the letter 'A' hanging from the post?—I want you to turn your horses to the left at the 'A,' toward the inside of the arena. Make a figure eight, please."

Ella grinned at the request. She'd make a figure eight on Figure Eight, all right!

Up ahead, Drew, who walked at the front of the line on his bay horse, reached the "A." He pulled his reins across his horse's neck and the horse turned, albeit slowly and stiffly, toward the middle of the arena.

Ash, who also struggled a little, went next, and then Jordan. She and Loco Roco moved through the turn flawlessly. This was obviously child's play for Jordan. Then Ella reached the "A."

Before she could even move the reins, Eight turned, following the path of the other horses, and headed across the arena. Ella frowned. She hadn't given Eight a signal of any kind—the horse seemed to be mimicking the others.

Ella let it go. It looked like she had done something, anyway, now that Eight was heading successfully through the figure-eight pattern. Neither Fletch nor Madison seemed to have noticed, because neither said anything to her.

"Hey!" Drew hollered from the other end of the arena. "Watch it!"

Ash, who'd been behind Ella, had cut completely across the arena and reversed. He passed Drew going the wrong way, bumping their legs together.

"You watch it," said Ash as he passed.

"You're going the wrong way, Ash," called Madison. "Turn around!"

Ash jerked his reins across his horse's neck, executing a sloppy turn.

When things were moving smoothly again, Fletch asked them for another figure eight at the opposite end of the arena. Again, before Ella and Eight had even reached the "C" sign on the far fencepost and Ella could tell her what to do, Eight was already turning. She headed smoothly across the arena and curved around the opposite end, making a perfect figure eight.

"Don't do that," Ella told her horse, quietly enough that nobody could hear. "Wait for me to tell you what to do."

Eight snorted as if she'd heard and didn't particularly care about Ella's preferences. Up ahead, Jordan rounded the curve and started to turn, gently pulling on the reins. She received an immediate response from Loco Roco, who coasted through the figure eight. Jordan said something to him, leaned forward, and patted his neck in praise.

A stone settled in Ella's stomach.

"Let's talk about using your body to help you turn," said Fletch. "Reins are only part of the bigger picture. The direction of your gaze, the angle of your body, and pressure from your legs all tell your horse what you want."

How could a horse tell where Ella was looking, when the horse was down there and she was up on its back?

"Everyone reverse at the 'A' again," Fletch continued. "But use your reins as little as possible. Look with your eyes where you want to go, angle your body, and apply a small amount of pressure with your outside leg."

It was a lot to keep in mind. Ella tried to remember

it all as Eight reached the "A" sign. Before Ella could give any commands, Eight did a flawless reverse.

"No!" cried Ella.

Madison glanced over. "What's wrong, Ella?"

"She's not listening to me."

"It looks like she reversed just fine," said Madison.

"But I didn't tell her to do it!" Ella's voice cracked with frustration, but she breathed deeply to calm herself. "Figure Eight did it on her own."

Madison considered that and then raised her hands. "Everyone, please stop for a moment. Remember, sit back in your seat, say 'Whoa,' and pull back on the reins."

The second Madison said "stop," Eight ground to a halt—before Ella could put any pressure on the reins at all.

Ella frowned. Sure enough, Eight was listening to the trainers, not to her. Not in the least.

CHAPTER FIVE

"**E**veryone stay stopped for a moment," said Madison in the center of the ring. She gestured to Ella. "Ella, tell Eight to go forward."

Before Ella could kick, Eight started to walk forward.

"Stop it," said Ella, yanking back on her reins. Eight kept walking. "Whoa! Whoa!"

Eight did finally stop, three steps later.

"Ask her to back up," said Madison. "Those same three steps."

But Eight was already backing up before Ella could ask for it.

"Agh!" cried Ella. "She keeps doing it!"

"It's okay, Ella," said Madison. "I won't speak

this time. Wait a moment, then ask again for the three steps."

After Madison had been quiet for a while, Ella pulled the reins tightly, sat back in her saddle, and shouted, "Back!"

Eight jerked her head, trying to free herself from Ella's iron grip on the reins. But Ella wasn't going to let her get her way that easily. "Back!" she said again, tightening her hold and pulling even more against Eight's mouth, and following it up with a firm kick.

"Not so forcefully," said Madison.

"But she won't do it otherwise," said Ella. The frustration grew and blossomed, turning her chest hot.

"Your arms are too high," said Madison. "Keep your elbows level with your hips. Pull straight back with the reins, not up by your shoulders." She turned to Jordan. "Could you demonstrate for us, Jordan?"

Jordan nodded. She dropped her elbows down by her sides, holding the reins in her fingers the way Ella's dad held the brakes when he took out his road bike. She gave a tiny tug, saying, "Back."

Loco Roco immediately took a step back.

"See the way she gives the command?" asked Madison. "Gentle tug with the fingers, elbows down."

"Sure," said Ella, but she had only half been

paying attention—too mad at Figure Eight to focus. Ella was going to make this horse listen to her.

Squaring up her shoulders, Ella yanked back on the reins, saying louder, "Back up!" Figure Eight resisted again.

"Back up!" Ella cried.

"Take it easy," said Fletch, approaching. "No need to yell."

"She's not listening!" Tears of frustration filled Ella's eyes. She couldn't cry. Just thinking about crying in front of everyone, on the first day of riding lessons, made anger boil up again.

"Let's let it go, then," said Fletch gently, and even the calm patience in his voice made Ella angrier, like he was condescending to her. "Everyone, resume a walk. Remember to stay on the rail."

Again, before Ella could even give the command to start again, Eight began walking.

"NO!" Ella shouted, yanking hard on the reins. "STOP!"

Then the angry tears broke loose.

"Ella, calm down," said Fletch again, then immediately looked like he regretted saying it.

"You calm down!" Ella roared at him. Then she turned back to Eight's reins in her hands and started yelling, "Back!" Now that she understood this was a remedial tactic for a horse that overstepped, she was going to use it. "Back!"

"Ella!" Fletch was at her side before she could blink and grabbed the reins away from her. "Stop right now. I will not allow you to treat your horse this way."

"She's the one who won't do what I tell her!" Tears rolled down Ella's face. The humiliation made her vision red. Even Jordan looked horrified, perhaps even ashamed for her.

Ella hated her for that look.

"Get off," said Fletch, his voice hard and stern. "Right now."

Ella climbed haphazardly out of the saddle, turned, and raced out of the arena, back to the bunkhouse.

\\\

No one came after her, which made the fury bubble up even higher. Shouldn't someone care that she'd stormed off in a huff?

But no one followed her to the bunkhouse, where she crawled up onto her bunk and cried angry tears into her pillow. The one time she thought she heard somebody coming to check on her, she raised her head—but realized it was only chickens scuffling outside. When she looked down, she saw she'd left wet splotches on the fabric in the exact shape of her face.

When she was all cried out, Ella simply lay there, staring up at the ceiling with crusty, reddened eyes. What a disaster this day had been. What a disaster this whole camp was.

Outside, she heard the other kids pass by her window—arguing about something or other, Madison trying to quiet them down.

When they were gone, Ella crept to the bunk-house door and peeked out. Her stomach grumbled. Everyone was probably heading in to help fix lunch.

Ella slipped out the door and followed behind them, staying out of sight. The three boys blundered inside the mudroom at the back of the house, and Jordan followed in their wake. Ella stood outside, trying to decide whether she should go in and eat lunch with everyone like nothing was wrong, or mope for a while longer.

Voices—different ones, older ones—floated out an open window on the side of the house. Right away she recognized Mr. Bridle's deep rumble.

Creeping up to the window, Ella scanned inside. There was a little office with a desk, a computer, and a spinning chair. The door sat closed, but the window was cracked to let in fresh air. Fletch, Madison, Ma Etty, and Mr. Bridle stood in a circle, heads bent together.

"This is the toughest group I've ever worked with," said Ma Etty. "In the twenty years we've been running this program, I've never had kids who had so much difficulty . . . settling in."

"It's only the second day," said Mr. Bridle. But he shook his head anyway. "Sure has been a tough two days, though, I'll give ya that, Etty."

Ma Etty sighed. "I don't know what we were thinking, putting them all in the same group. So many strong personalities—we should have known they would clash."

"Can't know anything like that in advance," said Fletch. "We did the best we could. We are doing our best, still. And we will for the next six weeks." He said it with no question in his voice, as if once camp had begun, he'd see it through to the last minute.

Ma Etty nodded. "Somehow, they need to see

that they're in this together." She rubbed her chin. "That they're on a team, not opposing forces. It's not a competition. It's a cooperation."

Madison sounded defeated as she said, "But, Ma Etty, it doesn't even seem like they like horses all that much." Ella sank lower under the windowsill, guilt turning her stomach sour. "Except Jordan."

Ella had really messed up—and now Jordan looked even more glittery and perfect.

As the group stood in morose silence, Ma Etty's head popped up like a gopher coming out of a hole. Her eyes glittered.

"That's it!"

The other three stared at her like she'd grown an extra arm. "What's it?" asked Madison.

"The horses are the reason we're all here," Ma Etty said proudly. "We just need to remind these kids of that fact. They came because they wanted to ride, because they felt a connection with horses. And that connection will bring those kids together."

Even Mr. Bridle sounded baffled by Ma Etty's train of thought. "They already had a lesson today," he said.

"It didn't go well," added Madison.

"I know, I know. Just listen. Fletch—what inspired you to pursue horsemanship seriously?"

Fletch scratched his head at the obvious question. "Well, George Fletcher. Bronc riding. As soon as I saw those old photographs, I knew what I wanted to be."

"Exactly." Ma Etty's entire face lit up. "Let's take them to a rodeo."

Madison still looked like she wasn't following, but the delight had spread to Fletch, too.

"The rodeo!"

"Yep. The Steamboat County Fair is happening right now. We'll have to make some phone calls to get permission, but we can do it. Those kids take one look at true horsemanship, and things will change. You'll see. If it could turn your life around, Fletch, it can do the same for others. Everyone can see themselves in the rodeo."

Ella backed away from the window. Ma Etty thought she'd be surprising them with this great news. Ella couldn't afford to miss acting excited, and hopefully fix what she'd messed up with Fletch and Madison.

She scurried around the side of the house and went in the front door, where the other kids had already taken seats around the table and were now bickering over when lunch was going to come out. All except Jordan, of course, who sat picking dirt out from under her fingernails, unperturbed by the disorder.

When Ella sat down, everyone went silent. She knew this silence. It was the same silence that had greeted Ella at the lunch table after she hit Bianca square in the mouth for that snide comment about her hair. It was the silence of people who would now tread more carefully, afraid of what they might do or say to set her off next.

Ella liked and hated this feeling equally. Now they'd never be her real friends—but they'd also avoid pushing her buttons. It was a tenuous compromise.

Soon Madison and Fletch returned, followed by Ma Etty with steaming cast-iron pans full of fajita fixings. No one remarked on Ella's reappearance.

When lunch was over, Ma Etty called for everyone's attention.

"I have a surprise for you!" she said gleefully.

"A surprise?" Kim's lips puckered. "I don't like surprises."

But no one could bring Ma Etty's mood down. "We're going to the rodeo," she said, smiling more to herself than to them. At the word *rodeo*, Jordan's chin snapped up.

"A rodeo?" said Ash. "Sweet." Then he added, "Wait, what happens at a rodeo?"

Drew laughed. "And Dallas calls himself a Cowboys fan!"

CHAPTER SIX

Ma Etty set a dress code for her ranch kids heading to the rodeo, so after Ella and Jordan finished packing up their day packs, Madison gave them button-up shirts that were a little too big but served fine with the sleeves rolled up.

"Oh!" Madison said. "One more thing!" Diving back into her room, she rummaged around before returning with two big cowboy hats, which she gleefully stuck on their heads. She grinned at Ella and Jordan with pride, then put on her own hat just as they were readying to leave.

"Let's get along, dogies," she said in a low cowboy voice, swaggering as she walked, and both Ella and Jordan cracked up as she led them out of the bunkhouse to the waiting van.

It was a junky old thing, but with Fletch at the wheel, it got them safely to the fairgrounds. Ella had never seen so many cowboy hats in a single place. Drew gave a running commentary of every new thing he saw. "Those cows have huge horns!" "Whoa, that horse is as big as an elephant." "What kind of saddle is that?" "Those guys are riding without bridles or halters or anything! How do they do it?"

No one bothered shushing him anymore. Eventually the van pulled into a parking spot and stopped. They unloaded from the van, and the loud, bustling rodeo unfolded around them.

There was an event at every building in the county fair, and at every moment, some audience was hooting and hollering. Right at the entrance, in a long, oval-shaped arena, a woman stood in front of a horse, the two of them staring at each other like rivals before a duel. The woman dropped to one knee, and to the kids' amazement, so did the horse. Then she dropped to both knees, and the horse followed so it was bowing before her. Then, they both shot up to their feet again, and spun in matching circles, to roaring applause.

"Wow," said Drew, and that seemed to be all he could say. For a moment, none of the kids spoke. Then Ash clapped his hands together.

"I didn't know horses could do that! This rodeo thing is going to kill my friends back home. I gotta remember to take pictures."

In her peripheral vision, Ella glimpsed Ma Etty's mischievous grin.

After the show, the kids split up, allowed to wander in pairs ("Use the buddy system!" Ma Etty said) as long as they were all back at the meeting point by one for lunch.

Unable to stand any of his fellow campers for a moment longer, Kim left with quiet old Mr. Bridle to watch calf roping. Ash and Drew, always hungry for thrills, went to see the bronc riding that Fletch had talked so much about on the ride over. Fletch and Madison left to check out the livestock, leaving Jordan and Ella to pair up.

What luck. Ella wanted a partner like Madison, who'd at least speak to her. But Jordan didn't seem to care either way where she ended up, and when Ella prompted her about what she wanted to do, Jordan shrugged, pointed, and said, "Let's go that way, I guess."

So they took off toward the covered arena, where shouts echoed under the aluminum roof.

People had packed the bleachers to popping. Ella and Jordan found seats way down in the middle. They had a lame view, stuck behind a guy who was at least seven feet tall. At Ella's grouching Jordan said, "Let's stay for a little bit, and if it's boring, we'll go find something else to do."

This was the most words they'd exchanged since arriving at the ranch, so Ella took it. She still wanted to know about those worn-out riding boots, to assess her competition.

Then Jordan said, "Look—over there, in the starting pen."

On the other end of the arena, a woman in a red shirt and cowboy hat rode a big brown horse through the gate.

"What a gorgeous quarter horse," Jordan murmured. The horse looked a lot like Figure Eight in shape, Ella thought, even though the color was different. Its neck was thick at the base, the chest full and shaped like a barrel, and the hindquarters so muscular they appeared almost square. When the excited horse moved, raring to gallop forward into the ring, all its honed muscles rippled.

Then, suddenly, the horse and its rider were off. Hooves roared into the arena. The rider's hat flew off immediately, letting her black braid swing behind her, and the crowd around Ella and Jordan burst into laughter.

Three tall barrels, arranged in a triangular pattern, waited for the competitors in the back center of the arena. She blazed straight toward them.

The woman and her horse turned so fast and so tight around the first barrel that Ella stood up quickly, thinking they might fall over, wanting to make sure she didn't miss it. They ran around the second, then to the third in the back, and galloped toward home at a speed Ella had never seen an animal go in real life.

"Seventeen point seven three seconds!" an announcer's voice boomed over the PA. "A fantastic showing from Missy Elwood and her stallion, Achilles!"

Applause rattled the metal bleachers, and Ella covered her ears as she waited for it to die down.

Then the next contestant entered the ring.

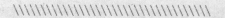

Ella's eyes never once left the arena as another woman came out on a beautiful yellow horse with a white mane and tail, the yellow splotched a little like watercolor.

"Ooh," said Jordan. "Definitely a full quarter horse. Must be. And that beautiful palomino coloring."

Ella could see what she meant now by 'quarter horse.' This animal was built long and thick and sturdy like the last one, with the same pretty, square jaw and full nose as Figure Eight.

"Do most people ride quarter horses in this event?" Ella said, hating the ignorance in her voice. But even her dad had to take classes on new subjects sometimes, had to ask his colleagues questions.

Jordan nodded. "Quarter horses are the best breed for barrel racing. They're good at the quick turn because of those huge haunches, and those super-fast starts."

Barrel racing. That's what this event was. Ella returned her attention to the woman and her yellow horse.

After a brief wait, they shot into the arena just like the first competitor had, straight toward the first barrel. They wrapped around it like a snake, tilting toward the ground in order to make the sharp turn.

Once the woman and her horse had gone most of the way around the first barrel, they galloped on to the second, speeding around it at an even more ridiculous cut than they had the previous one. Sweat coursed down the palomino's thick chest.

A timer was counting up, approaching ten seconds. Horse and rider got so close to the last barrel that her boot tapped the side. It tipped precariously. The crowd, Ella included, took in a collective breath.

The rider galloped on, speeding toward the exit—all while the barrel continued to tip. But as the competitor raced out of the ring, it became clear the toe-tap had been minor and the barrel righted itself.

A cheer burst from the audience.

"Narrow escape," said Jordan.

Ella couldn't help asking, "Escape from what?"

"Knocking over a barrel is a five-second penalty."

"That's harsh," Ella said. That was basically an automatic loss.

How did Jordan know something like that?

Ella and Jordan didn't agree on it out loud, but it was clear after they'd watched four competitors that they were staying to watch the rest. Ella wanted to know who would secure the fastest time.

Each rider seemed better than the last—quicker, more daring, making even tighter turns. One was penalized for knocking over a barrel, another for missing a barrel and going around it the wrong way.

"How do they turn like that?" Ella whispered to no one in particular. The riders hardly used their reins, it seemed. How did the horse know what to do?

"See their thighs and knees?" Jordan pointed at a rider heading out into the arena. "All the cues come through the legs. They're really bending their horses around the barrels—putting pressure on the front inside with the knee, to make the body curve in toward the barrel on the approach."

Jordan sounded so smart as she talked about this. Ella was impressed.

"As you get close to the barrel, you apply pressure with your leg on the outside, and pull the reins the way you want to go." Jordan gestured to illustrate. "That forces the horse to curve away from the pressure but keep moving in the same direction as the reins. It wraps the whole horse around the barrel."

As Ella watched the next rider, she saw in action what Jordan had explained: the rider's hands gently urged the neck around the barrel, while the outside leg pressed the horse into the optimal curve, then the inside leg straightened them out again as they pushed off to the next barrel.

It was mastery of horsemanship, pure elegance in the saddle.

Ella had to say what she kept wondering. "How do you know all this, Jordan?"

Jordan shrugged. "Somebody told me. A smart woman I know."

Ella gave her a skeptical side-glance, but when Jordan offered no other explanation, Ella decided to take her word for it.

"They're so fast—I didn't expect that." Another rider came out and tore around the cloverleaf pattern. Ella found herself grinning hugely. "I love it."

Jordan smiled. "Yeah," she said. "Me too."

They both stood in awe of the performance, sharing silence amid the tinny clang of feet on the bleachers and cheers from the audience.

Barrel racing.

Ella wondered if this was something that she could do. It was a perfect balance of skill and speed, technique and thrill.

"How hard is it to learn barrel racing?" Ella asked.

Jordan gazed into the arena. "Not hard. The pattern's simple. It's the technique that's difficult to master." They watched the final competitor take the barrels at a speed that looked almost dangerous. The horse snorted with each labored breath as they galloped home. "Like anything, I guess, it takes time and dedication to be really good at it."

Ella nodded, but she was already picturing herself atop one of those big horses, hat flying off her head as they cornered a barrel at a risky, heart-pumping speed.

"You know," said Jordan, surprising Ella by continuing on unprompted, "I heard Figure Eight has a long quarter horse lineage. Her build is perfect for barrel racing. If you wanted to learn, I think you'd be all set on a horse like that."

Her words went straight to Ella's heart.

"You think?" Ella asked. "Figure Eight?"

"Absolutely. Maybe she's been trained to do it already. Who knows?" Jordan smiled again.

Two smiles in one day? Ella wondered if something was wrong.

CHAPTER SEVEN

Ella couldn't contain her excitement the rest of the rodeo. They had funnel cakes and threw darts at balloons, but as they stood eating ice cream by a game Ash was spending all of his money on, she said, "The barrels were the coolest thing at this rodeo." She glanced at Jordan. "Wasn't it, Jordan?"

Jordan stared back at her, like a deer caught in oncoming headlights. "Uh, sure."

"Don't say that yet, Ella," said Fletch, breaking into a grin, like he knew a big secret that she didn't. "You haven't seen the team roping yet."

In the afternoon competition, quarter horses again headlined the show. Fletch and Madison pointed out the colors and breeds they could recognize as the teams lined up to rope their steer.

Drew let out a hoot as the event started and the steer was let free. The front rider got ahold of him by the horns with a huge lasso, and he and his horse together pulled the steer in a half-circle so its hind legs were exposed. The second rider raced up behind him, lassoing the steer's legs. His horse planted its feet firmly, pulling the rope taut, and the creature was immobilized.

It all happened in a matter of seconds. Everyone cheered.

But all Ella could think about was racing around those barrels, pinning her turns as tightly as physics would allow, and tearing up dirt as she and Figure Eight sprinted back to home base. The crowd roared in adulation, stamping the bleachers.

Now that they were reunited with the group, Jordan sank quietly into the background. But talk spilled out of everyone else on the ride home.

"Fletch," said Ash, "is it hard to be a bronc rider?"

"Sort of," said Fletch. "At least, being a good bronc rider is hard. You have to have guts."

"I want to try it!"

"When you get a little older, why not?"

"Bronc riding looks like a good way to break

your neck," said Kim. "I'm going to teach my horse to do tricks, like that bowing horse we saw. Things that don't involve getting thrown down and stomped by a bucking bronc."

"Me too," said Drew. "I want my horse to bow like that. But I want to ride the broncs, too. I'd hang on real well. I'm great at hanging on. And I want to split up the cows! That looked like so much fun. Is it hard? I want to try before camp is over."

Ella couldn't wait for lessons tomorrow, either. She was going to ask Madison about learning to barrel race. Like Jordan said, Figure Eight was built to run the cloverleaf pattern. Ella imagined the crowd again, roaring, whooping, cheering for her and her beautiful horse. It was up to Ella to fulfill both of their destinies.

That night, Ella was asleep before she was all the way under the covers, and she dreamed of hooves kicking up clouds of dust.

\\

The next morning, Jordan beat Ella awake again, and was gone before anyone else got out of bed. Jordan left her bunk a mess of blankets and sheets—as it always was, no matter how many times Madison told them to make their beds.

So Ella decided against going looking for Jordan, already knowing where she'd find her. If Jordan wanted to get up early and spend time with her horse, why not get special permission to ride solo? She'd easily get it. The trainers trusted her.

Instead, Ella put on her shoes and got down to the pasture so she could watch the sun come up. Even though the mantra was her dad's—*early to bed, early to rise*—Ella's mom had been the one to actually live it. When Ella was younger and her mom still lived with them, Mom was the one who'd get up at the crack of dawn just to watch the sun rise. When Ella climbed out of bed early to watch cartoons, she'd find her mom already awake, a mug of coffee in her hand, gazing out the kitchen window at the orange horizon.

Ella wondered what Mom would think of this ranch. She'd probably never find out, though, because Ella made a point of not calling her mom anymore. She hated when Mom popped into her thoughts like this, and she didn't want to encourage it. It was just like Mom to barge in and dump a bunch of feelings on Ella, without even being there in person.

Because thoughts like that—those wistful, pointless longings like *Mom would think this place is amazing*—were a distraction. They were the kind of thing Ella's dad warned her to avoid.

Have a couple school friends, he said, *but don't spend too much time with them and neglect your homework. Friends can be distractions.* Distractions from the big picture, from getting what you want.

Mom hadn't been the kind of person who was the best at anything, the way Ella and her dad were. Mom was mostly just okay at a lot of things. Maybe that was why she left. Maybe being around someone like Dad all the time was too hard. She'd sure had a lot more friends than he did, though.

A noise startled Ella. Someone else was hanging around the pasture, too. Ella scanned up and down the fence until she spotted Jordan, sitting on the top of the pasture fence, hidden from casual observation by the shadow of some stacked hay bales. She must have seen Ella long ago, Ella thought, and not said anything. How did Jordan blend in like that?

Neither of them greeted the other. At first, the silence made Ella itch with discomfort. She wanted to ask Jordan a million questions about why she was so strange, and how she was so good at horseback riding.

But Ella was unwilling to shatter the crystalline quiet that radiated from Jordan like a shield.

After a few minutes, Ella forgot what she'd wanted to say anyway, and got lost in the way the shifting light broke over the trees. She wasn't sure how much time had passed when they heard Madison calling their names. But Jordan climbed down from the fence, still not speaking, and Ella clambered down after her. Then the two girls silently headed inside for breakfast.

\\

On the way out to the barn for lessons, Ella was bouncing on the balls of her feet, thinking all over again about the riders roaring past at the rodeo, hats flying off, tearing turns around the barrels. The kids took turns tacking up as usual, until it came time for Ella to get Eight out of her stall.

"Actually," said Madison, stopping her. She pointed to a closer stall door, "you're riding Lacey today."

"What?" asked Ella, voice breaking.

Madison opened the stall and started buckling a halter onto the little brown pony inside.

"I've got you on a new horse," Madison said.

"Lacey may be small, but she's willing and fun to ride. You'll like her a lot, I think."

Ella felt like she'd been kicked. No—kicked and then punched. Then stabbed right through the chest.

"What about Figure Eight?" Ella asked, her voice rising an octave as Madison put Lacey into cross-ties. "I'm supposed to ride Figure Eight."

"I figured with Eight giving you so much trouble last time, we'd get you up to speed on the basics with Lacey, since she's a little more forgiving. Then, when you've gotten the hang of riding, we'll put you back on Figure Eight."

The image in Ella's mind—of tearing around a barrel at maximum velocity with Figure Eight—burst into flames.

"No." Ella glared at the little bay pony patiently waiting to be brushed. "No way. You can't do this to me."

A crease appeared on Madison's forehead. "Do what to you? Lacey is a fantastic pony. She'll teach you a lot."

"I don't want that horse!" cried Ella. "I want Figure Eight. I want my horse back."

"Well," said Madison, turning her back to Ella, "that's too bad. You've proven you can't keep your temper in check with Figure Eight, so I had to pair you with a different horse. If you show that you can be patient—"

"NO!" Ella roared, slamming one fist into the stall door. It rattled the metal bars up and down the barn, startling the horses.

"Hey now," said Madison, stepping toward Ella. "None of that in here."

"You can't!" Ella wailed, angry tears slipping down her face. How could Madison do this to her? Figure Eight was hers! They had a destiny to fulfill. "No! It's not fair!"

With a sob of anger, Ella kicked a plastic barrel full of horse biscuits. It went spinning across the floor, surprising Lacey.

"Ella Pierson." Ma Etty's stern voice sliced the air. "Get out of my barn. *Now.*"

CHAPTER EIGHT

The deep laugh-lines on Ma Etty's face were, for the first time that Ella had seen, completely devoid of laughter. The old lady's bright eyes had turned to ice as she regarded Ella.

Ella's temper flared, like a bonfire with new tinder. Who did she think she was, kicking Ella out of the barn? She was about to object to the humiliation, but Madison said, "I'll put Lacey back."

With no horse to ride, there was no point in Ella still standing there, so she crossed her arms and stomped outside. Ma Etty followed her and slowly, calmly, closed the barn doors behind them.

"How dare you?" demanded Ella. The old lady had actually kicked her out!

Ma Etty's lips were a thin line. "Luckily, Lacey is such a good pony she didn't spook when you kicked over those biscuits—but what if your carelessness had frightened her, and she hurt herself? Or hurt Madison? What about all of my horses who are now distressed because some young lady, who should know better, threw a toddler's temper tantrum in my barn?" The old lady stared Ella down. "I'm the one who should be saying 'How dare you.'"

Ella wanted to scream, to punch that retort right out of Ma Etty's mouth. At the thought, she jammed her hands into her jean pockets and bit her lip as hard as she could.

But Ma Etty didn't look afraid, the way everyone else did when Ella started thinking about socking someone in the mug. Ella had deduced that it showed on her face when she was about to punch, because most people got fear in their eyes and backed away.

Ma Etty only raised her eyebrows at Ella— almost, Ella thought, like a taunt.

That poured cold water over her fire. She would never hit an old lady, not ever. Ella glared bitterly at the ground as the rage melted off into tears.

"There now," said Ma Etty, leading Ella over to the bench next to the barn, where observers could watch activity out in the arena. "Feel better?"

Ella wiped at her face, wishing she was not crying in front of Ma Etty. The embarrassment made her angry all over again.

"No," said Ella crossly. "I don't feel better. You took away my horse. I want to ride Figure Eight. I want to barrel race."

That made Ma Etty sit up a little straighter. "Barrel race?" Her mouth curved up on one side. "Oh, I see. Did you and Jordan see the barrel racing at the rodeo?"

Ella nodded silently, sniffling.

"Interesting." Ma Etty *hmm*ed, looking out over the other kids and their horses as they did warm-up laps. "Well, I see why you threw a little fit over Madison pairing you up with Lacey. Figure Eight is the perfect horse for running barrels." She *hmm*ed again, and Ella felt her temper erupt once more at Ma Etty's calmness. It annoyed Ella how the old lady always seemed totally in control of herself, in a way Ella never was.

"If she's so perfect for it, then why can't I ride her?" demanded Ella.

"Good question," said Ma Etty. "Why can't you?"

Ella glared at her for tossing the question back. But Ma Etty sat patiently, awaiting an answer.

"Because you won't let me," Ella finally said.

"Even if I did let you, you'd still have trouble riding her. You might even throw a tantrum again, like at your last lesson. What's different now that you can suddenly ride a horse you couldn't ride before?"

"I want to barrel race now," said Ella. "I have to." Figure Eight would sense this immense shift in Ella's priorities, she was sure. And Eight would respond to her determination. They had a destiny to run those barrels together.

"I ask again," said Ma Etty, "what's different now? Just because you want to do something far off in the future doesn't change the fact that, as of this second, at your current skill level, you cannot ride Figure Eight without losing your temper."

This roundabout discussion made Ella want to scream. "Far off in the future?" she said. "I could start learning to barrel race today, this second, if you let me ride Eight!"

"No, you couldn't."

There was no room in that cool tone for argument. Ella felt like a bug squashed under a very large shoe.

"What do you mean, I can't?" Ella croaked. Her fantasy of Eight's hooves eating the dirt, of the cheering crowd in the stands, was dying.

"From what you saw at the rodeo, did barrel racing look easy?"

Ella was about to respond with an instant *yes, obviously*, when she thought about those steep, knee-to-the-ground turns. She remembered what Jordan had said about using knees and thighs together to wrap the horse's body so tightly around the barrel. "Well, no . . ."

"Let's say Figure Eight already knows how to run a cloverleaf pattern," Ma Etty said, though her tone carefully didn't give away whether or not this was the case. "Do you think that right now, you could barrel race and not hurt yourself? That you'd have even a chance of telling Eight what to do, and of her listening to you, after your last lesson?"

Ella didn't speak, but she shut her eyes and rubbed her palms against them, attempting to stave off more tears.

"I'm not trying to make you feel bad, but expert-level barrel racing takes years of hard work and training," Ma Etty went on. "But most of all, it requires an incredible degree of trust between horse and rider. And at the skill level you are now, what reason does Figure Eight have to trust you?"

"I can work hard," said Ella, with all the force she had inside her small body. That was the one thing she knew she could do: put herself to a task and work at it until she'd won, until she'd figured it out, until she'd hammered and clawed her way through every obstacle in her path. "I can work hard enough to do anything I want."

As she heard herself saying it, Ella thought, *That's what Dad always says, too.* That made her mad again.

"With horses," said Ma Etty, "just working harder isn't enough."

Ella couldn't imagine a problem that couldn't be solved by working a few more hours, trying a new tack.

"It takes patience," Ma Etty went on. "Kindness. Compassion. Thoughtfulness."

Not Ella's usual tools for success. But like anything, she figured, if she worked at it, Ella would bet money she could get good at them. She'd be the most patient, the most kind, the most compassionate—if that meant getting Figure Eight back.

"And when I have those things?" Ella asked. "When I'm thoughtful and compassionate and whatever, can I ride Figure Eight again? Learn to barrel race?"

Ma Etty raised both eyebrows.

"Ride Lacey," she said. "Stick with her for a while. Prove to me you're not just a good rider—that's required, too—but that you're a patient rider. A kind and sensitive rider."

"How do I prove that?" Ella asked, annoyed.

"I get regular progress reports from Fletch and Madison," said Ma Etty. "When you've got that temper under control, we'll talk again." She stood up. "Then you should ask Jordan for help with the barrel racing part."

"Jordan?" Ella frowned.

"She won first place at the California Junior Rodeo last year. She's an expert barrel racer—plus, she has a fantastic knack for horses. There's a lot you could learn from her, Ella."

This information stunned Ella so completely, she couldn't say anything for almost a minute. Her thoughts raced as she looked out into the arena, where the other kids were working on their posture. Jordan, with her little brown pony-tail waving behind her, checked her heels along with everyone else.

How do you know all this, Jordan?

Somebody told me. A smart woman I know.

Jordan had lied to her.

\\

Even after her talk with Ma Etty, Ella was still banned from the barn for the rest of the day, so she hung around outside kicking rocks and thinking.

First place at the California Junior Rodeo. What a whopper to keep secret. Why? If Ella had won something like that, it would have been the first thing she said at introductions.

When Madison handed out their chores, Ella found she'd been paired up with Jordan in the chicken coop. What luck. Now Ella had a chance to interrogate her.

Why had Jordan said someone told her about the finer points of racing, when really, she was an expert in her own right?

Ella wanted to expose Jordan, make a chip in her perfect image, and call her out on such a bald-faced lie.

But Ella remembered she already had one strike against her, so as angry as she was, she decided not to speak to Jordan . . . yet. She might say something that would get herself in trouble again.

In the chicken yard, Ma Etty gave the girls a run-down of their duties, and finished by saying, "Now, these chickens are my babies. Treat them like you would treat, well, someone's babies." She stooped, patted a chicken on the head, and said, "Sesame Seed here is my favorite, but don't tell Dumpling." Then she left them to it.

They gathered the eggs in silence, startling a few chickens still sitting on them. After off-loading the basket in the kitchen, they returned to refill the chicken feeder and check the water level.

Finally, as they started sweeping out the chicken coop, Ella couldn't hold it in any longer.

"What's your deal?" she said, halting her broom.

Jordan looked up. "What?"

"You lied to me, Jordan."

Her eyebrows knitted together. "Did I? I don't remember—"

"About knowing how to barrel race." Ella gave a short, bitter laugh. "Ma Etty told me that you won a barrel racing championship. Why didn't you tell me?"

The color drained from Jordan's high cheekbones.

"O-oh," she said. "That."

"'Oh that'?" Ella mocked. "That's all you have to say?"

"It . . . it was just a fluke." Jordan clutched her broom handle. "It wasn't me at all. It was Mrs. Rose's horse, Antonio."

Ella crossed her arms. "Who's Mrs. Rose?"

"A real nice lady who lives down the road from me," said Jordan, looking anywhere but at Ella. "She lets me ride Antonio sometimes. He's . . . he's a really fantastic animal." Jordan's hands trembled as she started sweeping again, avoiding meeting Ella's gaze by staring hard at the broom handle. "Antonio knows the barrels by heart. Just runs them on his own. I don't even have to do anything, besides hold onto the reins and lean forward."

"You're trying to tell me a horse won a championship for you?"

Jordan nodded rapidly. She got the broom stuck in a cranny and pulled on it, but her movements were sloppy and distracted.

"Like I said, I don't know a lot about barrel racing. But Antonio is the whole package. He loves the barrels, you know? He'd run them even if I wasn't on his back. Loves the thrill—eats it up. Especially once people start yelling and cheering, he's a big ham."

Ella let this wash over her, because as unlikely as it sounded, she could imagine a smart horse like Figure Eight acting like that, too. But Ella couldn't believe Jordan had nothing at all to do with winning a regional championship.

"You knew all that stuff about barrel racing at the rodeo," said Ella. "You must be kind of good at it."

Jordan gave her trademark shrug. "Mrs. Rose taught me a little, and lets me exercise her horses for her after school. When she suggested I compete on Antonio because he loves the spotlight, I agreed. That's all. It was just good luck, and Antonio."

"Then why did you come here?" asked Ella, her tone accusatory, feeling she still had something to be mad at Jordan about, that there was still some inherent deceit. "I thought this place was for kids who wanted to learn how to ride, not for people who are already good at it."

"I . . ." Jordan swallowed, her eyes never leaving the floor. "Ma Etty said it was fine. My parents thought that since, you know, I've had one good thing happen to me on a horse, that coming here would be good for me. That it would teach me focus, or determination, or something." She sucked in a big breath, and she gave Ella the impression of a vase, perched precariously on the edge of a shelf, about to tip over and smash on the ground. "I only came here because my parents sent me. It wasn't my choice, you know."

She said this last part almost angrily, and turned her head away, cradling the broom handle to her chest.

That made it a little better to Ella, that Jordan had been sent here against her will. She felt sympathetic to that, also having a strong-willed parent.

"How long have you been riding?" asked Ella, incredibly curious now about how this shy, quiet girl had won a championship. "How did you hook up with this lady, Mrs. Rose?"

But Jordan stared at the floor, sweeping the same spot she'd swept five times already. "Not long," was all she said.

After that, Ella couldn't wiggle even one more word out of Jordan—only grunts and shrugs and head shakes. Ella regretted calling her a liar, because now Jordan wouldn't even look Ella in the eye.

They spent the rest of the afternoon cleaning the chicken coop in total silence. If only she hadn't slammed the door to Jordan McAdam, just as it was starting to open.

CHAPTER NINE

Ella had her dad's persistence, so she didn't let what had happened with Jordan trouble her. The next day during the morning riding lesson, she threw herself into becoming the best horsewoman she could, even though she had to ride snooze-fest Lacey.

And as Ma Etty had suggested, Lacey did listen to Ella. Whenever Ella asked, Lacey walked or turned or backed up around the orange cones Fletch had arranged. The rodeo seemed to have worked a bit of magic on the other kids too, because all their attention was focused on speeding up to a trot. Ella watched Fletch and Madison's faces, wondering if this step was enough, and when they'd report back to Ma Etty that she was ready to ride Figure Eight again.

Probably not, though. Ella had a feeling that impressing Ma Etty wouldn't be easy.

Ella and Lacey were walking directly behind Jordan and Loco Roco. Ella hated watching them, the way they seemed to work in perfect tandem, like two halves of the same whole. He anticipated her commands, often sliding to a smooth stop before she could say "Whoa." Jordan barely looked like she was doing anything to get sharp turns and careful, snakelike bends around orange cones.

As Ella watched Jordan silently sway in her saddle, moving in perfect rhythm with Loco's walk, she wondered if Ma Etty's prescription could actually work—if Ella could ever become the kind of horsewoman that Jordan was.

\\\

Ella got paired up with Kim that afternoon for chores, and though she'd dreaded it during lunch, it turned out that Kim was good company. He kept to himself unless he had a sarcastic remark to make, like, "You'd think this fly would get the hint after the fifth time I've almost smacked him." There wasn't much glory in gardening—just a lot of dirt. Ella wanted to complain, but she didn't.

Patience. Kindness. Compassion. Thoughtfulness. She kept repeating the words in her head.

She tried the thoughtfulness part out while they worked, but it was deadly boring. She couldn't think about anything except how badly she wanted to be racing around those barrels on Figure Eight's back.

Saturday was supposed to be blazing hot, so Fletch and Madison planned a ride out into the wilderness that bordered the ranch, where the trees and the mountains would keep them cool.

Ella wanted to ask about taking Eight, because they'd just be plodding along at a walk the whole time, but she remembered: *patience*. Ugh.

As the kids gathered with their horses in the gravel parking lot for the ride, baking under the hot sun, a man rode a huge horse down Bridlemile Road from the northern end of the ranch. Ella had heard from Drew that the Bridles grazed cattle up there.

The man had windswept blond hair and a bushy mustache. His enormous horse, colored the strangest deep brownish-red, stopped in front of them. Three handsome, black-and-white dogs trailed along behind.

"Paul, glad you could make it," said Madison,

waving from the ground. "Think you can handle this group?"

Paul emitted a bellyful of laughter. "Handle?" he said. "Who needs handlin', Maddie? We're just gonna go walk through some woods and enjoy the scenery together."

At this, Madison stifled a laugh. "All right then," she said, and then waved to the kids. "Paul here is the ranch manager at Quartz Creek Ranch, and he offered to lead your trail ride today. Fletch and I are staying here to catch up on exercising our own horses. So please listen to Paul as if he were us." She paused, then said, "Scratch that. Don't listen to him as if he were us. Listen to him as if he were a two-hundred-pound man who knows how to fire a rifle through a coyote's heart at three hundred yards. That's more accurate."

Paul gave her a perplexed look, but Madison just winked and sauntered off.

"Okay then," said Paul, pointing off toward the green mountains lying to the west of them. "Let's go!"

\\\

"This all is White River National Forest," said Paul, gesturing grandly at the blue-green trees sprouting up all around them as they wound uphill, into the woods. "One of the prettiest darn places in the whole wide world, if you ask me."

"I don't remember asking," said Kim near the back, so only Ella, Drew, and Jordan could hear. Ella and Drew both chuckled.

"What's that back there?" called Paul.

"Nothing," said Kim. "Just agreeing with you."

"Hmm," said Paul.

That made Drew and Ella giggle even harder. Jordan, who followed behind Kim at the very back, stayed silent. It reminded Ella about her pledge to Ma Etty, and her own laughter tapered off.

How was she going to master any of the traits that old lady wanted? Kind people were like Jordan, like Mom. They went quiet and looked away when the conversation turned against them. They didn't fight for themselves. They were doormats.

And people like Ella, people like Dad, who were willing to step on and over those doormats—those were the people who made it ahead in this world. Who got what they wanted.

There had to be another way of becoming the

type of horsewoman who was allowed to ride the beautiful, graceful, powerful Figure Eight.

Then, as Ella turned her head to take in the trees passing by, she spotted Jordan and Loco Roco in her peripheral vision.

A thought struck. Ella needed a teacher, like Ma Etty had suggested—someone who had what she was missing. Someone who had the trust of Fletch, Madison, and most importantly, Ma Etty.

Ella leaned back in her saddle and whispered to Kim, "Hey, trade places with me?"

He arched an eyebrow at her, but then he shrugged. "Whatever," he said and passed her in line, putting Ella just in front of Jordan. Ella could practically feel the other girl tense up behind her.

This was one benefit of Lacey, Ella thought, as she turned all the way around in her saddle so she could face Jordan. Lacey kept moving just behind Kim's horse, taking no notice of her rider's misbehavior—or if she did notice, she didn't care at all.

"What's up?" Ella asked. She realized as soon as she said it how lame it was.

Jordan just looked at her posture with wide eyes, and then looked away.

With a sigh, Ella sat normally in her seat again

and pulled back on Lacey's reins. Confused, but ever willing, Lacey slowed down so Loco Roco could catch up to her. Then they continued on, side by side, a few paces behind the rest of the group, as Paul began telling a long-winded story.

"Good work in the arena the other day," said Ella. "You know, when we . . . walked around."

Man. Ella could not seem to stop with the lameness.

"Uh," said Jordan, "thanks."

"How long have you been riding horses?" Ella asked, trying out this question for the second time now.

"Um . . . two years, maybe three?" Jordan shrugged.

That's what she always did, it seemed like—shrug as if she didn't know a single thing in the world, as if she had no authority on anything, including how long she'd been riding horses.

"How could you not know?" Ella asked with a chuckle, before she could think better of it.

Jordan's lips pressed together and she answered with silence, and another shrug.

This was going about as poorly as Ella's original plan to get Eight back. She didn't know how to talk to someone like Jordan. She could volley easily with someone like Dad—someone who believed completely in his abilities, sometimes beyond them. Nothing Ella said could chip his armor or make him think less of himself. Sometimes Ella hated that.

But then, she also could never hurt him by accident. So they made an okay team.

Or they did after Mom left. She could never take that stuff—too delicate, Dad said. Sometimes, during the divorce proceedings, he had called her a wimp. Thin-skinned. Fragile. Even though Ella had decided to stay with her dad when they went to court, she'd never been able to decide if she agreed with that assessment of Mom or not.

Maybe Mom just didn't like having her confidence and patience tested every moment of every day.

"Sorry," said Ella after a long while had passed. Jordan had kept pace with her and Lacey.

Jordan gave her a strange look. "For what?"

"For what I said. For being sarcastic."

Jordan shrugged. Again.

"Jeez," said Ella. "Don't you feel things besides 'I don't know' or 'I don't care'? Like, didn't that annoy you, that I said that?"

Another shrug. Jordan started slowing her horse down, falling behind again.

"What are you gals doing back there?" called

Paul from the front. "I don't want you to fall behind and get lost."

Ella sighed. This wasn't going to work. "Okay," Ella called back. "On my way, Captain." She gave Lacey a little kick to catch up with the others, leaving Jordan alone in the back. Probably the way she wanted it.

Up at the front, Paul regaled the kids with a tale of the time a cow escaped onto the neighbors' property. Neighbors who—from what Ella could tell this far into it—were pretty mean, grouchy people. Worried what might befall one of his prize heifers, Paul had bemoaned the pickle his cow found herself in to a previous group of ranch kids. They heroically marched in after her, rescuing her, and barely escaped with their lives. At least, that was how Paul told it.

"That's a dumb story," said Ash. "Something like that would never happen at this ranch."

Paul frowned. "Well, that's rude. It did happen— I saw it. I was there."

"Uh huh," said Ash, rolling his eyes. He always had to take somebody down with him.

"Shut up, Ash," Ella said. "I liked Paul's story. Well told. Very dramatic." She even clapped a little.

Paul frowned. "I'm pleased to hear that, Ella. But no telling people to shut up on my watch either, okay?"

Ella sighed. "Okay."

The dogs had found a bone as they ran circles around the slow-moving horses, and they were taking turns carrying it around. Soon, Paul slowed down and said, "Here we go."

The forest opened up before them. Hills rolled out below, the edges tinged blue-green. The immense, snow-capped Rockies took over the skyline.

Paul turned away from them to focus on the path as he began talking. "This part of White River is known for its natural spring water," he started saying.

Ash and Drew were whispering and giggling. In the two seconds Ella had been gazing out at the scenery, Drew climbed up in his saddle so he was half-standing on top of his horse, like one of the trick riders at the rodeo. Ash was on his way to the same position. When he saw she was watching, Ash gave Ella a challenging look.

"What? Gonna throw a fit about it?" he said quietly. The dare to join them went unspoken.

If there was any horse you could pull a stunt like this on, it was little Lacey. Ella felt enormous pride in her boring, constant pony as she got onto her knees first, grabbing the horn with one hand for balance. It would be a shame if Paul turned around, she thought briefly. Lacey didn't bother with whatever Ella was doing and kept walking.

Drew had gotten all the way up on his feet, looking back at Ella, when Ella saw a low-hanging branch just ahead of him. She pointed, mouthing, "Duck!"

But instead of doing as she instructed, Drew turned to see. The branch hit him across the side of the face. He started sliding off his horse with comical slowness as both the branch he'd run into and the steady, slow pace of his horse radically delayed his fall.

Paul decided right then to turn and ask them a question.

"What on God's green Earth?" he cried. He flipped his horse around and jogged back down the line. Ella slid back properly into her saddle. Drew's horse, sensing he was losing his rider, abruptly halted.

This motion sent Drew sliding all the way off, still desperately clutching the tree branch, and he dropped unceremoniously onto the ground. The dogs ran up to Drew, yapping and licking, and he laughed as he pushed them away. He didn't look hurt in the least, maybe a bit dirty.

"That was the dumbest thing I have ever seen," Paul said, his expression somewhere between astounded and furious. "Who tries to stand up on their saddle? Were you raised in a barn?"

"Obviously not," piped up Kim. "If he had been, he might know better."

Drew stood up and dusted himself off, sheepishly taking his horse by the reins. "Hey," he said. "Worked out better than that joyride I took on my bike, at least."

"And you two," Paul said to Ash and Ella. "Motor-mouth is one thing, but the two of you!" He couldn't even seem to find words for how angry he was.

Ella opened her mouth to say something, to explain herself somehow, but Paul raised his hand to stop her. "No," he said. "Don't say anything. We're going back. Now."

A gasp rose up from the very back of the train of kids, and Ella was sure it had been Jordan.

"But we've only been out here—" said Ash.

"Back!" Paul hollered. "Now!"

No one spoke as they turned around and headed back down the hill toward Quartz Creek. Paul rode at the head of the line, no longer full of stories. Even his horse walked more stiffly, and his dogs took up what seemed like guard positions all along the line of kids, no longer playing or arguing over bones.

Ella fell in line behind Jordan this time. The other girl looked absolutely miserable as they stalked back down the mountain and onto the ranch land. It really was hot out, Ella thought, so heading back down to the ranch was a bummer. But it wasn't like Jordan had done anything wrong up there. What was eating her?

CHAPTER TEN

"**W**e're back!" Paul hollered gruffly as they rode back into the parking lot.

Fletch poked his head out the office window. "So soon?"

"So soon," Paul confirmed. "I don't want injured campers on my watch, you know what I mean?"

"Injured campers?" Fletch sighed and ducked back into the office. After some scuffling, Madison and Fletch both came out the front door and helped the kids off their horses. They didn't bother to ask what had happened, and Paul didn't tell them.

He stuck two fingers in his mouth, let out a sharp whistle to call his dogs to him, and galloped off on his big blood bay, back the way he'd come earlier that morning.

Why did Ash and Drew have to ruin everything? That stupid trick-riding idea had obviously been Drew's, and Ash shouldn't have challenged her.

Where Ella had missed the heat up in the forest, down on the ranch it was dry and suffocating. Even the grass seemed wilted and brown. They sat on it as they ate their lunches, because they hadn't been gone long enough to eat them on the trail ride.

"Man," said Jordan. Everyone turned to look at her when she spoke. It was the first time she'd ever done so freely. "We could have been swimming right now."

"Swimming?" asked Ella. "Where?"

"Fletch mentioned a glacial lake up there, on the trail."

"Glacial lake?" Drew asked with his mouth full of food, then swallowed it. "Like the kind that's so clear you can see to the bottom?"

"Yeah," Jordan said.

"Whatever," said Ash. "It probably wasn't that cool. All lakes look the same."

Ella felt so outraged at this that she couldn't even bring herself to speak at first. There had been a gorgeous glacial lake waiting as their final destination, and they'd missed it?

"Wow," said Ella sarcastically. "Thanks a lot, Drew."

"Hey," said Ash. "You got up there too. Wasn't just Drew."

Ella wanted to argue with him, but there was no point. So the kids fell quiet and ate the rest of their food in silence, baking in the afternoon sun.

\\

After the morning's events, and an afternoon sweating and toiling in the heat, everyone came to dinner grumpy and tired. As plates were handed around, they bickered over who had taken more than their fair share of Ma Etty's stew, and the tension in the room swelled.

The hot food was exactly the opposite of what Ella wanted to be eating right now, but she spooned more into her bowl anyway. She was famished. Her clothes stuck to every square inch of her because she'd been sweating so much. Why didn't the Bridles have A/C if the summers here got this bad?

"Hmm," said Kim, stirring his food with a pinched look on his face. "Totally overcooked."

Ma Etty didn't even look offended. "Happens," she said.

"You shouldn't cook meat for so long," Kim went on. "Makes it carcinogenic. Can give you cancer. When my mom makes Korean food, she cooks the meat real fast, in boiling water. It tastes a lot better."

"I'll try to remember that," said Ma Etty, even giving Kim a little smile that annoyed Ella.

"Nobody asked you, Kimberly," said Ella. The talk of boiling water in this heat made her feel sick. Or maybe she just wanted Kim to shut up. "Stop bragging."

"Ella," said Madison. "Respect."

"What?" Ella demanded. "He's insulting Ma Etty's cooking and going on about how Korean food is better, and you're telling *me* to show respect?"

"It's true that it's not healthy to overcook things," said Ma Etty, as if just to show she wasn't injured and didn't need Ella to defend her. "You lose good nutrients."

"My dad's Irish," said Ash. "They overcook everything! It's so gross. I hate family reunions."

Ella directed her annoyance into cutting a big piece of gristly meat. She wanted Ash and Kim to stop talking because Ella had nothing to contribute. Mom had left before Ella was old enough to learn about Indonesian cooking. All she knew was that it used a lot of hot peppers.

"You guys are lucky," said Jordan, who watched her bowl while she spoke. "There's no traditional food in my family. Well, besides sloppy joes and hot dogs. And my mom puts mayonnaise on everything."

"All-American, huh?" said Drew. "My mom's family are all from South Carolina, and they take their barbecue sauce seriously there. At least we have some heirloom barbecue sauce recipes."

"'At least'?" said Ella, bristling. Drew, of all people, making fun of Jordan? "Who cares about barbecue sauce?"

Fletch put down his knife. "Come on, now, guys. Everyone can be proud of where they came from and the food their families make. Jordan, I ate the same kind of stuff as you growing up. It's definitely All-American."

"Broke American, you mean," said Kim under his breath.

"Kim!" said Ma Etty, the patience in her voice evaporating. "What is with you all tonight?"

Ella glanced at Jordan as she went back to eating. Her face was red.

Kim was probably right. Jordan didn't seem to have much money, but she had made it work. She'd even managed to get a regular gig riding horses—and probably not by taking expensive riding lessons.

Ella glared down into her food and stirred.

\\\

Sunday was supposed to be another group activity, but before the day had even begun, Ash and Kim were already yelling at each other over the last pancake. Ash picked up a tin cup full of maple syrup and hurled it at Kim, hitting him in the head and spilling sticky, slippery syrup all over his hair, the wall behind him, the table, and the floor.

Mr. Bridle got to his feet and slammed his utensils down on the table with a resounding clang.

"That's it!" he said, huge voice filling the dining room. The boys ducked back into their seats. "I've had enough. That incident yesterday with Paul, then the insults at dinner last night, and now this?" He took a long, calming breath. Ella felt dread curl up in her stomach. Even Mr. Bridle's tolerance appeared stretched to its limit.

"Everyone is going to be separated this afternoon," he said finally, wiping his lips with his napkin. "All chores, all day. No partners."

"What?" cried Drew.

"And," Mr. Bridle continued, as if nobody had spoken, "I'll be teaching lessons tomorrow. You're off, Fletch and Maddie. Feel free to take a trail ride, or go help Paul's boys with the new calves, or whatever you want to do with your free time."

Neither of the trainers actually looked pleased about this, but they nodded and said nothing.

Had this happened before, that Mr. Bridle took over teaching? It seemed unlikely. Ella saw him as the sort of guy who sat quietly and did paperwork, or fielded phone calls and marketed the ranch to parents. Not the sort to get in front of kids and teach.

A spike of fear ran through her. And, looking at the other kids' faces, she wasn't the only one.

They'd really, truly messed up.

Sunday was another sweaty, hot day, and this time, Ella had to suffer through it alone.

First, Ma Etty showed her how to milk the goats and then left her to do every single nanny goat alone—all nine of them. By the end, her wrists and hands felt like lead weights, and one of the nannies, whose teat she'd pulled on too hard, had kicked her in the thigh.

Then, after lunch, Ella mucked stalls. All. Afternoon.

"This should be illegal," Ella said to herself, since there was no one else around to complain to. "This is indentured child labor. This is illegal, I know it."

But nobody cared, because nobody could hear her.

For the first hour, Ella repeated her complaints to herself, until even her own voice annoyed her. So she stopped talking at all.

When the complaining ceased, she seemed to find a rhythm: stick the fork-rake-thing under the poop, tilt it back up to keep as much poop on the rake as possible while lifting it, then toss the poop into the wheelbarrow. Occasionally, as she went to dump each wheelbarrow of manure onto the manure pile behind the barn, she caught sight of the horses out in the pasture.

They couldn't look more pleased with the sunny weather, or the day off. They chased one another, flinging their manes around, running back and forth like puppies playing in a yard—even sweet Lacey, who she'd said such mean things about, was romping with the others.

What a jerk Ella had been.

Happy, at least, that the horses were having fun when she couldn't, Ella went back inside with the wheelbarrow to fill it again. Her sore arms cried out, *No more poop! Not another wheelbarrow!*

And yet, there was more poop. There was always more poop.

By late afternoon, Ella had reached a meditative state. Stick the poop, lift the poop, toss the poop. She even stopped swiping at the bugs, because she felt bad for killing them. They were just trying to live too.

Ella lost track of time, no longer caring whether her punishment ever ended. She was starting to think she deserved it.

She deserved it for yelling at Figure Eight.

Ella wheeled out another load of poop and dumped it, stopping for a moment to wipe sweat from her forehead and gaze up at the fiery sun.

No wonder Jordan avoided her. Ella had mistreated her own horse. Ella would avoid somebody like that herself.

Ugh. And then Ella had gone and called Jordan a liar, too.

Once she got thinking about it, Ella found her list of sins was long: She'd egged Kim on at dinner. She'd punched Bianca at school.

Ella looked down at the wheelbarrow, and shame crept up in her chest.

She'd chosen Dad over Mom.

And she'd let Mom leave. Her kind, loving mother . . . Ella had let Mom go without even telling her she loved her.

As Ella headed back into the barn, tears starting to work their silent way down her cheeks, a blaze of white and fawn-brown shot across the pasture.

Ella blinked, rubbing her eyes.

Figure Eight galloped from one fence to the other, bucking and swinging her head. She looked utterly magnificent, that painted horse, frolicking in the green grass under the sunshine. As Ella watched, she couldn't even feel angry at Madison and Ma Etty anymore for taking Figure Eight away. She just felt joy watching her.

"Ella!" She turned at the sound of Ma Etty's voice. "Come on inside! It's time for dinner."

Ella had a vaguely disappointed feeling. She'd miss the predictability of the stick-lift-dump, because who knew what trouble might erupt at the dinner table?

Ella sighed, put down her rake and wheelbarrow, and followed Ma Etty inside.

\\

But she had nothing to fear. The others were all just as tired as she was, and hardly anyone said a word during dinner. Afterward, the kids stumbled back to their bunkhouses like zombies.

As the girls went inside to change out of their dirty, sweaty clothes, Jordan held up a hand with her palm facing Ella. At first, Ella was so tired that she didn't understand what was happening. Eventually she raised her own hand and met Jordan's high-five, smiling.

"You're alive," Jordan said, grinning in that unguarded way only total exhaustion can bring.

"So are you!" Ella laughed, suddenly giddy. Jordan had chosen to approach her. Jordan had talked to her. Even high-fived her!

The girls high-fived again at the fact they had both survived the day, and that was the last thing that Ella remembered before she dragged her numb body into bed.

CHAPTER ELEVEN

Everyone was slow to breakfast in the morning, and there wasn't much talking.

Ella figured their penance wasn't over yet.

She knew about penance. When Mom still lived with them, she made Ella attend mass with her every Sunday. Keeping still and silent for that long was hard even for some of the adults, but Ella had learned how to daydream while still looking attentive as the priest droned on.

She'd learned how to confess, too. How to say her rosaries to make up for each mistake she'd made during the week.

It seemed all the kids at the table knew they were finally saying their rosaries today.

When breakfast was over, Mr. Bridle got up, hat so low it partially covered his eyes. He folded his napkin and set it on the table.

"Let's go."

Quietly, the kids got up out of their seats and followed Mr. Bridle out to the barn. He dragged out five wooden saddle stands, each with a student's saddle already on it.

"Get on up," he said. Ella saw Kim bite back a sarcastic remark, and he climbed up on his saddle on the wooden horse with everyone else.

Mr. Bridle meticulously corrected their feet, their knees, their legs, their seats—even their shoulders. He never raised his voice, never needing to. And when they were done, he put them on their real horses and made them walk around the arena for what felt like hours, doing the same thing. He nitpicked everything about their posture, their seat, their feet, their attitude.

"Your horse feels what you feel," he said in his deep, mahogany voice. Ash chuckled and Mr. Bridle said, "What about a thousand pounds of lean muscle and the power to read your mind is laughable to you, Ash?"

Ash's smile fell away. "Uh," he managed.

"You get on there thinking this is a joke," said

Mr. Bridle, "and what's your horse to think? That this is just a game for him, too? That's a horse that doesn't back up when you ask, because he thinks you're a clown for his amusement."

Ash flushed red.

Next, Mr. Bridle picked on their hands, making them do figure eights around the arena, one after another, never changing speed. If a horse slowed down or sped up, Mr. Bridle jumped on the rider.

"Why is your horse moving faster right now?" he'd say. "Bring it back down." The horses were just as bored with the endless walking around the arena as the kids were, and would sometimes try to start jogging.

Ella started to feel when Lacey was about to speed up, usually when she sensed the horse in front of her start to trot. Ella would adjust her posture to match, sending her weight back in the saddle and giving Lacey a tug on her mouth with the reins.

"Don't pull so hard, Ella," called Mr. Bridle, and Ella hated how he seemed to see every single thing she did. "Small motions. Whispering, not yelling, not unless Lacey ignores you and you need to yell."

Obediently, Ella tried out using smaller, precise

motions. When she did, Lacey paid closer attention and would listen to Ella's quiet requests right away.

Ella focused on getting better at this, keeping in constant contact with Lacey about what speed she wanted, about how close to the rail they should be.

"Tell them with your eyes where you want them to go," Mr. Bridle would say, over and over, as they cut across the arena one way, then the other, then back again. "You should be twenty-five feet ahead of your horse at any time. Look at the top of the fence posts. Pick the one twenty-five feet ahead of you and stare at it. Then the next one. Then the next one."

He was right. Ella found if she looked where she wanted Lacey to go before she signaled her to turn, it didn't take much pressure on the corresponding rein to make her turn. It was as if Lacey got the sense, long in advance, of what Ella wanted, what she was going to ask—then prepared herself to do it.

Ella thought of Jordan's Antonio, Mrs. Rose's horse.

Mr. Bridle stopped them for lunch, and the kids fed and cared for their horses before eating. Ma Etty brought out burritos so they wouldn't have to leave for too long. As they stood in the cool, dim barn, silent except for the rustling of paper burrito wrappers, Kim pointed at Jordan and started laughing.

"You got some sour cream on your pants," he said. "And it looks exactly like Mr. Bridle's head."

Everyone stopped to peer down at the sour cream stain.

"You're right," Ella said. "It looks just like Mr. Bridle's head. The big hat, the square chin—it's even got his ears."

As they all stood gaping, Jordan wiped it off, leaving a wet splotch on her jeans. Ash laughed. "Still looks like Mr. Bridle's head."

"You should go inside and have Ma Etty wash that off for you," said Ella, "so they don't stain."

Jordan shrugged. "No biggie. These old jeans are so beat-up, you won't notice later. They were already pretty ratty when I inherited them from Olly. Anyway, I'm up to get a new pair next month." She smiled at this.

Kim turned away at this information about Jordan. His cheeks flushed pink, while Jordan just picked at the stain thoughtfully. So even Kim could regret being so mean to her the other day.

Ella finally broke the silence. "I really like your jeans, Jordan," she said. "I thought you got them from a thrift store back home. I love thrifting. I mean, why buy new stuff when there's plenty of great used stuff out there?"

Jordan shrugged. "I guess."

"I buy almost all my stuff thrift," said Kim suddenly. His face was still red as he pulled the collar of his GI Joe shirt out to show them. "This is my favorite find ever. Vintage. Very rare."

This was probably the closest to an apology Jordan would get from Kim.

"What do you know about T-shirts?" asked Ash, snickering.

"A lot. I collect them." Kim grinned. "What about you, Dallas? You do anything interesting besides rabid fanboying over your favorite football team?"

Ash wiped his mouth and balled up his empty wrapper. "Yeah. Art. I do art."

"Art?" asked Drew, leaning in. "Like what?"

Ash lowered his voice as he said, "Street art. That's why I'm here."

"You got caught tagging something?"

Ash barked a laugh. "Tagging is for noobs. My buddy Cruiser and I were at my house one night and made this amazing wheat-paste piece."

Ella stared at him. "Where was your mom?"

"She's a waitress. She works late. So Cruiser and I take it a couple blocks down and start putting it up—"

"You did it near your house?" said Drew, covering his mouth.

"Sure. There's a lot of art where I live. Anyway, we'd just gotten most of the Cowboy up when the cops caught us."

"You were putting up *Cowboys* graffiti?" asked Jordan. Even she looked aghast.

"Yeah, of course. Why?"

Jordan just shook her head, and Drew laughed so hard he had to sit down.

"It was a work of genius," Ash said wistfully. "And nobody but us ever saw it."

\\

After lunch, Mr. Bridle drilled them about pieces of tack, care and grooming, even horse anatomy. Once they'd parroted back to him all the facts and techniques he wanted, they got back on their horses and worked in the pasture. It was harder to control the horses out here, at least for Ash, Drew, and Kim. Lacey was too compliant to be much trouble, and Jordan had a perfect handle on Loco Roco.

"Keep your legs back, Ella," Mr. Bridle said as they made circles in the grass around him. "Heels down—no, that's too much. Let them fall naturally; don't shove them down. Press the balls of your feet into the stirrup, and the rest follows."

Why couldn't Ella do it right? There were too many things to track and control: your hip, your leg, your heel and your toes, and that was before you'd gotten to just holding onto your reins right.

"I'm trying," said Ella.

"Your elbows are sticking out," said Mr. Bridle. "Elbows down by your hips. Reins right in front of you, not out over the horn."

"I'm trying!" It was too much to focus on at once. She couldn't manage it all in her brain.

In Ella's frustration, a quiet thought occurred to her. Nobody was arguing. Nobody was mocking one another. Mr. Bridle had forced all of them to focus so much on their horses, on their seats, on their hands and their feet, that they had nothing left for squabbling. And slowly, they were starting to improve.

Unfortunately, still always at a walk.

Yet it had stopped being boring. Now Ella could see what she was doing wrong—why sitting incorrectly in her saddle, even just a fraction, could make a big difference. She saw it in the two laps she did sitting stiffly in her saddle, then the following two, where she sat down and back, like Mr. Bridle kept telling her.

So she worked on correcting the tiny imperfections that showed themselves as Lacey walked and walked and walked. She could feel Lacey's mouth now through the rein, and kept it just taut enough that a small movement of her finger brought an instant response.

"See, Ella?" called Mr. Bridle. "It's all in the whisper, not the yell."

Ella knew what he meant now. The more quietly she "whispered" to Lacey what she wanted, the more Lacey was willing to give it to her. By the end, Ella hardly had to move to request a turn or to hug the rail closer. She and Lacey shared the same goal.

When the day was up, Ella was reluctant to get off Lacey's back, as much as her thighs hurt. She'd gotten so used to riding that she felt like the pony's four legs belonged to her more than her own two did.

Now, in addition to her arms aching from mucking the day before, Ella's legs burned from thigh to ankle. All the kids walked like they were made of Jell-O.

"This is abuse," Kim muttered as they headed to the ranch house for dinner, tripping over chickens in the yard that they were too tired to step over. "I know it is. It has to be."

"We signed up for this," Ella said.

"Not me," said Ash. "My mom was the one who picked cowboy camp. She has a weird sense of humor."

"I think Ella means us acting like idiots," said Drew. Ella had to give him credit—even he was acting a little more perceptive after their lesson.

"Oh, yeah." Ash sighed. "That's annoying, isn't it."

No one had a response to that, because before that lesson with Mr. Bridle, it was hard to say that any of them except Jordan had been taking horse camp all that seriously.

"Sorry you had to go through that with us," Ella said to Jordan. "You haven't really caused any trouble at all."

Jordan gave her usual shrug, but this time, Ella thought that was nice of her not to say anything. She could have gotten mad at them for dragging her into this, and she'd have had every right to.

But she didn't.

That night around the dinner table, Madison and Fletch were in a chatty, boisterous mood after their day off. Mr. Bridle seemed to have decided that, with penance over and the day's grueling lesson at a close, he could return to his usual jovial, quiet self. He offered the kids rolls with butter slathered on them, baked potatoes, turkey and gravy, and even cranberry sauce.

"Thanksgiving in August?" asked Kim, pouring gravy over every single thing on his plate until it was swimming.

"That's a lot of food, Kim," said Madison. "I hope it doesn't all go to the compost."

"Oh," he said, "don't worry. I'm going to eat all of it."

"Thanksgiving in August," agreed Ma Etty. "Why not? You kids need the protein after the last two days."

At least she acknowledged how much work they'd done, Ella thought, and followed Kim's example with the gravy. The boy did understand food. Gravy on a crescent roll, with butter also, was the best thing ever.

Then, after dinner, it was strawberry rhubarb pie with vanilla ice cream, and the kids all thought they'd died and gone to heaven.

Even though it was Monday night, they didn't go back to their bunkhouses after dinner. "Everybody follow me," Fletch said, getting up from the table and looking a bit mischievous.

He led them out of the house and around to the side, where they found Paul already standing by the fire pit, warm flames billowing up from the tinder pile in front of him. Ella squealed in joy. Goofy Paul was back, and he didn't look the least bit mad at them as they took seats around the fire.

"Before you get too comfortable, let's take care of the important things," said Paul, and distributed two bottles of bug spray. The kids covered themselves in it from head to toe, at his urging. "Don't want you to wake up itching all over tomorrow! You don't see 'em now, but they're nasty little buggers after dark."

Madison, Ma Etty, and Mr. Bridle joined them with s'mores, passing out long sticks, chocolate, graham crackers, and two bags of giant marshmallows.

"Didn't we just have dessert?" Ella whispered to Jordan, hoping all the activity had put her in a conversational mood.

"You know what they say," whispered Jordan. "Don't look a gift horse in the mouth."

"Who says that?" asked Ella. "And why?"

Jordan laughed. "It's about being grateful for gifts. Someone gives you a horse, you don't look at its teeth right there to see if it's old. It's free. Be happy."

"I've always wondered what that meant." Ella grinned. "Thanks. You're pretty smart."

Jordan cracked half a smile, but stayed looking at the ground.

As they overlooked the few glimmering lights of the town of Quartz Creek, Paul pulled out a banjo that looked as old as Mr. Bridle. "This is an antique," he was eager to point out. "Real deerskin drum." He tapped the wide, round base of the instrument.

Ella expected some dreary old folk music, but the first song Paul played was a loud, fast, bluegrass song that made her feet tap. Ma Etty and Mr. Bridle must have felt the itch, too, because soon they were up on their feet dancing. They swung around, hands intertwined, like they were thirty years younger. Then Fletch and Madison joined them, and one of Paul's ranch hands who worked with the cows even pulled out a tiny drum to keep some rhythm.

Then Jordan got up, swinging a long imaginary

skirt around, twisting and twirling with the music in a country way Ella could only describe as highly experienced. Mr. Bridle whistled and the trainers started clapping. Soon Drew was up too, tossing himself all around like a puppet on a string. The ranch hand whooped. Then Ella was up and spinning in circles around the fire, unable to fight the music anymore, and Ash and Kim joined her.

After the dancing, Mr. Bridle told a surprisingly scary story that involved howling wolves that weren't really wolves—they were moon people, from an old legend about people that could turn into wolves and hunt at night. But then came strange foreigners who didn't understand. As Ella predicted, the foreigners tried to kill the moon people.

"And then," said Mr. Bridle, as a coyote with flawless timing yipped off in the distance, "the wolf came at him, and nearly bit off his face!"

Jordan and Kim both yelped as Mr. Bridle abruptly raised his voice and threw his hand out at them.

Later, Paul played some slow, soulful banjo songs that Ella liked even better than the fast ones. Within minutes Drew was half-asleep on Ash's shoulder, which made all the kids crack up. Ma Etty finally roused him and sent everyone off to bed.

"Easy day tomorrow," she promised.

"Oh good," said Kim as he waddled off to the boys' bunkhouse. "Only three hours of poop-scooping instead of five." Ella and Jordan both laughed as they made their way to their own bunk.

CHAPTER TWELVE

Ma Etty kept her promise.

"Free time," she said at breakfast. "All day." She held up a finger. "But any bickering, any at all, and the day resumes as normal. Horse lessons and chores and you-name-it."

The five of them nodded furiously.

"All right. Go forth, then, and have fun. There's a list of things you can do posted on the wall over there."

Ella scanned the list with the others—bean bag toss, Frisbee, music, and more. But the thing she was looking for wasn't there.

Learn barrel racing on Figure Eight.

Even the television was teasing her. Fletch and

Madison had put on the stock show in the living room, although they were sticking to the strict no–screen-time rule for campers. But the trainers kept dashing there and back to see riders they liked or livestock events that were interesting. From the dining room Ella could hear the announcer reeling off winning times in barrel racing.

As Ella stood in front of the list of activities, she wondered why even horseback riding wasn't on it. That was all she thought about doing these days. Wasn't it the same for everyone else?

She jumped when Madison tapped her shoulder.

"I want to talk to you."

Uh-oh. It sounded so ominous—but what had she done? Ella followed Madison outside, wondering what this was about.

Then they started heading to the barn in silence, and Ella's heart skipped a joyful beat.

Inside the barn, Madison stopped in front of Figure Eight's stall. Ella took a breath. She could only hope.

"Mr. Bridle spoke with me after your lesson yesterday," Madison said, leaning against the stall door.

"What . . . what did he say?" Ella asked, trying to keep her voice cool.

Finally, Madison grinned. "He said you were a natural. Working with Lacey has been good for you—but she's too easy. He told me to bump you back up to the big leagues." With that, she grabbed Figure Eight's halter off the hook and opened the stall door.

"Think you can handle working with Eight again?" Madison asked.

Ella's mouth fell open.

"Yes! Yes, please!" Ella wanted to bounce up and down, but she wasn't going to pull a Drew and scare Eight, just as they were getting paired up again. "I mean," Ella corrected herself, straightening up, "thanks, Madison."

"Thank Mr. Bridle," she said, handing Ella the halter. "Now show me what you can do."

\\

"I wasn't sure if a lesson was what you'd want to do with your day off, after the day you had yesterday," Madison said as Ella led Figure Eight out of her stall and put her in cross-ties.

"Ha!" Ella had to laugh at that. Throwing a Frisbee around didn't hold a candle to the possibility of riding Eight again—not to mention one-on-one instruction from Madison.

Out in the arena, climbing up on Eight was a completely different experience from getting on little Lacey. Ella could see everything with Eight's extra two hands of height. And Figure Eight felt different underneath her. Maybe it was her imagination, but Ella thought she could feel the horse's taut muscle through the seat of her saddle, could sense the power in her huge lungs.

Sitting on Eight's back felt, to Ella's immense satisfaction, like being inside an overfull hot air balloon, just waiting for someone to twist the valve and start the fire.

"Very good seat," Madison called. "Heels are perfect, your legs are back, and your shoulders are relaxed. Memorize that feeling, Ella. That's your go-to point. Now take her into a walk."

Eight tried to move forward at Madison's utterance of the word *walk*, but Ella said "Whoa" and tugged her backward. Eight reluctantly stopped.

Ella tried to remember everything she'd learned in Mr. Bridle's lesson. She drew her hands up to the spot in the reins where she had contact with Eight's mouth, but wasn't applying any actual pressure. Satisfied, Ella gave a single click of her tongue to start into a walk.

And Figure Eight listened.

At first, she refused to stay on the rail, pulling her head back toward the middle of the arena—and toward Madison.

"Correct her each time she tries that," said Madison, and Ella pulled Eight back to the rail.

On the other end of the arena, Eight cut the corner dramatically, and Ella corrected with another tug on the rein, toward the railing where she should have been walking. Eight straightened, but only a little.

"Use your inside leg to reinforce your request, if you need to," Madison called.

But Eight was wise to what Madison was saying, and she didn't cut any more corners. Now that Ella could see how shrewd Figure Eight was, she felt intimidated. This wasn't little Lacey anymore.

After a few laps Madison said, "She's done warming up. Take her to a trot."

At Ella's first small kick, Figure Eight hurtled into a lopsided canter. It tossed Ella to and fro, and she lost her gentle hold on the reins. One of her feet slipped out of its stirrup.

"Slow her back down," Madison called. "And don't let your legs go rogue like that. You're throwing her away just when she needs you to be firm. Show Eight she can put her trust in you."

That feeling returned of there being too many moving parts to control all at once. How could Ella keep her foot in the stirrup while flopping all over Eight's back?

Ella finally got Figure Eight back to a walk again, and they did another lap before attempting the trot a second time. She gave the signal—pressure on both of Eight's sides—and again, Eight leapt into a fast, bouncy, nervous canter.

"You're too tense," said Madison. "That's why Eight keeps trying to go fast. She thinks you want her to go fast."

Ella tried to relax, to soften her shoulders, but she was annoyed now. Not at Madison, though. She was irritated at herself. Why was this so hard?

She kicked for a trot again, but Eight wanted to run, and the loose reins whipped about like an attacking snake as Eight sped up again.

"Don't let go of your reins," said Madison. "Pull her back, Ella."

She was trying, but Eight wasn't listening to

her—again! Ella tried to breathe, but Eight was still lunging ahead.

Ella remembered Mr. Bridle's lesson: lower your elbows. Sit deep in the saddle. She focused on one aspect of her posture at a time. Suddenly, Eight's pace slowed. Ella applied a little more pressure to the reins, pulling them directly into her torso instead of up toward her neck, and Eight slowed down more— until she ambled along at a nice, even trot.

"There you go!" called Madison, giving her a thumbs-up from the middle of the arena. "Keep her at a trot. Relax more, Ella. You're trying too hard to match her gait, and that's why you're bouncing all over the place. Let your body match up to hers naturally."

Naturally? There was nothing natural about this motion. It hurt less at this speed, but Ella still couldn't stop bouncing. At this rate, she'd never get to a gallop, and she needed to gallop in order to run barrels.

"Relax!" Madison called to her. "You're so stiff."

"I'm trying!" But the bouncing only got worse. Why was she so bad at this? Relaxing should be the simplest thing in the world.

"You're even stiffer now." Madison went quiet

for a while as Ella and Eight bounced around the arena. Then Eight started speeding up again, her trot getting faster and rowdier. "Slow her down."

Ella jerked too hard and Eight slowed all the way down to a walk. At least now Ella could breathe again. Her whole body hurt. Why couldn't she do a simple trot right? Her annoyance at her own inexplicable lack of skill rose to full-blown anger.

"You've got to relax," said Madison as Eight continued at a walk, and Ella tried her hardest not to snap back with a retort. "You're bouncing because your hips and legs are fighting Eight's. You have to let your body synchronize with hers."

"Easier than it sounds!" Ella couldn't understand why riding Figure Eight was so hard for her. She'd been good at this yesterday.

She supposed she was actually a terrible horse-woman. Lacey was a beginner pony who had made Ella feel too comfortable.

"Here," Madison said, gesturing for Ella to return to the center of the ring and climb out of the saddle. Once Ella was off, Madison took her place on Eight's back in a quick jump.

Madison easily guided Eight back out to the fence. She gave a light kick. Eight, sensing she had a much more experienced person riding her who wouldn't put up with that jump-into-a-canter business, glided into a smooth, slow trot.

"This is what you're doing," Madison said. She went rigid, like a human iceberg, and immediately Eight's bouncy gait tossed her into the air. They bounced like that for a few steps and it made Ella's legs ache to watch. Eight's gait immediately changed and she lifted her head, looking unsettled.

"This is what you should be doing," Madison said. "See, I'm not stiff. I'm not forcing myself to move. I've just freed up my hips to move however Eight moves."

Something in her posture went slack, and Madison settled into the saddle like she was out in the car for a cruise. Her shoulders dropped forward, not so much that she was slouching, but enough that she looked at home—comfortable, even.

"Don't try to force a straight posture," Madison said as she and Eight sailed around the arena, her legs moving with the horse, her hips and stomach and shoulders all rising and falling at the same speed, in time with Eight's own motion. "No need to be nervous."

Pfft, Ella thought. *Don't be nervous.* How was

Ella supposed to feel, doing so badly in front of Madison?

"I'm not judging you," Madison went on, as if she could read Ella's mind. "I'll keep helping you until you figure it out."

"What if I never figure it out?" Ella asked sourly as Madison came back to the center of the arena.

"Don't worry," she said. "You will. Just give yourself the same leeway you gave Eight today."

"Leeway?"

"You were so patient with her!" Madison smiled as she hopped off Eight's back and handed the reins back over to Ella. "You corrected all her mistakes without getting mad. I was really proud of you."

"But I did so badly!" Ella's eyes burned. Madison had given her this great opportunity, offered to teach her on her off-time, and Ella had disappointed her.

"You did great," Madison said. "I don't know what you're talking about."

But the torrent came anyway. "I suck at this." Now that Ella had seen Madison in the saddle, so perfectly relaxed and comfortable and not bouncing around at all, she felt like even more of an epic failure. "I was supposed to be good at this, but I just really, really suck."

"Ella," Madison said, "you are learning. Everyone has to start somewhere. Cut yourself some slack."

But how could she? Yesterday, Ella had finally felt that connection to her horse, finally got a handle on all of the parts and pieces and they'd fit together so wonderfully. How come today, on the horse she'd dreamed about riding again, it had been so different?

"Eight is just so difficult to ride," said Ella, her eyes feeling wet and glassy.

Madison nodded, and did not suggest otherwise. "Every horse is different," she said. "You have to learn your way around each one individually. Just like with humans."

Ella had never thought about it like that. She glanced down at Eight's long, elegant, spotted neck, and ran a hand along it. Figure Eight dipped her head and leaned into Ella's arm.

If the two of them were ever going to race, Ella thought, she would have to figure out what made Eight tick.

CHAPTER THIRTEEN

Madison introduced them to the "gymkhana" events that week—which, to Ella's great pleasure, included barrel racing. They were events designed around obstacles like barrels and poles to help them develop handling. "And it's always fun to race," said Madison.

Everyone was excited to try them out after the rodeo. Madison asked Jordan to demonstrate each event at a trotting speed—pole-bending, where Jordan weaved Loco through a row of poles and back again. Then keyhole, where Jordan ran Loco inside a small square of poles, performed a loop, and sprinted home. And last but not least, they performed the cloverleaf barrel pattern—flawlessly.

Ella was so excited to try the barrels that by their turn, Figure Eight was dancing in place, sensing her impatience. Ella wanted to run the pattern, to take those sharp turns at a hard gallop like the racers at the rodeo. But she knew she hadn't reached that level with Eight yet, and without that connection to each other, Eight might just gallop off, out of control.

Ella couldn't afford to mess up again and have Eight taken away.

They were supposed to walk each pattern, but by the time they reached the barrels, Eight started off at a slow trot. Madison didn't object as they headed for the first barrel, but Ella was nervous after her last lesson.

Nevertheless, Eight seemed to be in a good mood out here. Her ears perked forward, toward the first barrel. Keeping that close contact with her through the reins, Ella focused on relaxing. She sank into the saddle and kept her eyes on the spot just to the left of the barrel—where she wanted Eight to go.

As the barrel came up on their right, Eight's neck bent underneath her, around the barrel. Still moving at a slow trot, they cleared it and headed to the second one.

Ella's gaze stayed twenty-five feet ahead of Eight.

She was thinking about going around the obstacle when Eight anticipated her. They cruised around the barrel, so close to the side Ella could have reached out and tapped it with her foot. She cheered inside her head.

Then, the last one. Another left turn. The other two had gone so well, she worried this was when Eight would decide to act up. As if in response, Eight tossed her head and sped up her trot, tossing Ella into the air.

"Relax!" Madison called. "You're tensing up!"

Ella let out a long breath and focused again on where she wanted to go: around the barrel. She barely had to tug on the rein for Figure Eight to wrap around it.

And then, they were clear.

Eight, her neck low, sped up her trot. She was just as eager as Ella to finish out with a bang. Deciding Eight had done a good enough job to warrant it, Ella let her go at a fast trot back to the end of the line, where the other horses were waiting their turns.

"Wow!" said Ash, flicking his blond bowl-cut out of his face. "You two looked sweet out there."

Drew's head bobbed up and down. "Totally sweet."

Madison rushed out into the arena. "See how Eight's neck dropped like that?" She grinned at Ella. "That was her relaxing. When you're calm, she's calm. She feels safe with you. That's what I like to see."

Ella tingled from neck to ankle. They'd done the barrels! Even if it was just at a trot.

But even better, Eight had trusted Ella. In that moment they'd moved as one unit, with one mind. Ella had thought, and looked, and Eight had followed.

Ella just hoped they could do it again tomorrow.

\\

But after that, they left the gymkhana events behind and returned to horsemanship. Ella's stomach dropped.

She'd wanted to gallop those barrels, and now she'd lost her chance. She wanted to scream, *Let me keep practicing them!* But Ella wanted to appear subdued, to show the old lady she had mastered those irritating virtues.

Anyway, when did she have time to practice? Ma Etty would never let her out of daily lessons with Fletch and Madison. Maybe she could use her free time. Ella would prefer riding anyway to Frisbee or bean bag toss or whatever else.

As soon as she had the idea, though, she knew she couldn't ask Figure Eight to work hard two times a day.

So Ella did something she never thought she'd do. As they were taking food scraps out to the compost after lunch, Ella asked Madison if she could be paired up with Lacey again.

"Really?" Madison upended her container of peels and eggshells over the fence. "But you and Eight are doing so well together. I don't understand."

"If I'm going to work Eight separately on the barrels, I can't be riding her all morning, too."

Madison frowned. "Work her separately on barrels?"

"Sure. I want to practice with her every day, for at least two hours. I'll spend half of it on the barrels and half of it on just horsemanship."

"Where will you find time for that?" Madison asked. "You still have to do your chores every day."

It was Ella's turn to look confused. "Free time, duh."

"So, let me get this straight. You're going to ride two hours a day on Lacey with Fletch and me, and then another two on your own time, with Eight?"

"Yeah, sure." Ella shrugged. "I'd rather do that

with my free time than play soccer. I'll do my chores, then go work with Eight."

"Who's supervising you?" Madison asked.

Ella hadn't considered that. She'd thought Mr. Bridle's recommendation would be enough. "No one," Ella said tentatively.

Madison bit her lip. "That won't work. And I can't be out there watching you myself because I have things I have to do around the ranch." She glanced at Fletch, who was at the table handing out chores. "Neither can Fletch. He's up to his ears in work helping Paul get ready for new yearlings to arrive next week." She thought for a moment. "Perhaps Mr. Bridle could help you. He has a little bit of barrel know-how. But you'd have to ask him—he's crunched for time, too."

The little lesson plan Ella had built in her head burned to the ground.

"But Madison . . . !" she said, as they headed back to the house. "Eight and I are doing so well together. We'll be fine alone."

This had always worked on her dad. All Ella had to say was, *I know I can do it. I'll make it happen, Dad.* And if she spoke in that confident tone of voice, he would smile at her and say, *Okay, Ell. Do it. Make it happen.* He liked her best when she acted like him.

Madison shook her head. "I'm sorry, I don't know what else to tell you."

"But—"

"Sorry," Madison said. "Not alone."

\\\

Ella wanted to break something.

She couldn't believe it—Madison turning her down like that. Ella tromped into the house with her boots still on. Ma Etty, who was sitting at the dining room table, raised her eyebrows.

"Ella, leave those boots in the mudroom."

Ella glanced down at her feet and practically snarled when she saw what she'd forgotten. She tore the boots off her feet and stalked back out again, dumping them in the mudroom. There she ran into Jordan, who was sliding hers off, too. Literally ran into her.

Their skulls knocked together and they both shouted, "Ow!" as they stumbled backward. Ella rubbed her head. Without thinking about it, Ella said, "Watch where you're going!"

Dang it. She always seemed to slip up around Jordan.

"Sorry," was all Jordan said, and she made sure

to right both of their pairs of boots by the door. "I'm sorry, I wasn't looking."

Ella wanted to roar something at her. *Stop apologizing! Have a backbone!* But getting mad at Jordan wouldn't accomplish anything. It might even set her back—though Ella wasn't sure how much farther back it was possible to go.

"It was my fault," Ella said. "I'm the one tromping around like a bull in a china shop."

Jordan glanced at her. "What's wrong?"

The question, and the eye contact, took Ella by surprise.

"Uh . . . I'm mad, I guess."

"About what?"

"Madison won't let me practice barrels during free time."

"Hmm." Jordan closed the door behind her and they walked together back toward the kitchen. "That's silly. You should get to do whatever you want with your free time. Though that is a lot of work in one day for Figure Eight."

"I know! So I told Madison I'd ride Lacey for lessons, and only work Eight in the afternoons."

Jordan's eyebrows knit together. "She shouldn't have a problem, then."

"She said nobody has time, except maybe Mr. Bridle." Then a thought occurred to Ella. "I think she doesn't trust me in the arena alone."

As soon as she said it, Ella realized it was true.

Jordan had an expression on her face like maybe she agreed with Madison on this assessment. If it had been anyone else, Ella would have socked them.

But Jordan was probably right. Ella hadn't exactly proven herself to be the most in-control around horses.

Then you should ask Jordan for help with the barrel racing part, Ma Etty had said.

Maybe that's what Ella needed: Jordan. The trainers trusted her. If Ella could get Jordan on her side, could get her to teach her the barrels, they would let her practice alone.

\\

During free time, Ma Etty decided to take them on a trip to see the new frogs that were starting to appear down at the creek. On the way home for dinner, Jordan fell to the back of the group as she usually did—and Ella followed her.

Ella didn't speak first, and Jordan didn't start a

conversation, either. Ella wanted to demand that Jordan become her teacher. But she knew where that would get her.

Instead, Ella waited. Then, after a while she said, "How's it going with Loco Roco?"

Jordan gave her a surprised look.

"He's a good horse," she said. "Smart, eager. Funny, too."

"Funny?"

"Yeah. He likes to nibble on my pockets when I turn my back to him, or play with his lead rope while we're tacking up. He has a good sense of humor."

Ella had never considered that a horse could have a sense of humor. But if anyone would know something like that, it would be the girl who spent her mornings quietly sitting with her horse in the barn.

"That's so cool," said Ella. She wished she had that kind of relationship with Figure Eight. It would probably make the riding part a lot easier. "Hey, I want to ask you something."

"Like what?" Jordan asked, giving her a sideways look. Ella barreled on, sensing that she needed to assure Jordan she didn't have a nefarious purpose, as Kim would say.

"I just want to learn how to run the barrels

properly," Ella told Jordan. "And you know how, right?"

"Well, sure," said Jordan. "But so do you."

"Not as well as you. You won a championship."

"It was a—"

Ella held up one hand. "I know you're going to say it was a fluke," she said. "But I've seen how you ride Loco Roco, and you're obviously better at this than I am, by a long shot." It wrenched Ella's gut to say it out loud, but there was no more obvious truth.

"I couldn't teach anyone," said Jordan, and Ella saw her clamming up again.

"Yes, you can!" Ella said it forcefully, with complete confidence, hoping her faith would be contagious—that Jordan would sop up some of it and keep it for herself.

"I don't know," said Jordan, hesitant. "I've never taught anyone anything. I could mess you up."

"No, you couldn't."

Jordan shrugged. "Who knows what I'm capable of?"

Frustrated, Ella wanted to try harder to convince Jordan that what Ella had said was the truth—Jordan couldn't mess anyone up. But she'd seen what that had done last time, so Ella went quiet as well. She just kept pace with Jordan, as if agreeing to the silence.

Jordan's anxiety seemed to fade as they approached the house. As they started heading inside, Jordan stopped on the stairs. Even though she didn't look at Ella, Ella knew she was talking to her when she said, "I'll maybe think about it, okay?"

Ella nodded and said patiently, "Okay."

"It still doesn't guarantee we'll get permission to practice alone," said Jordan.

"I know," said Ella. "That's okay. I just want to try."

CHAPTER FOURTEEN

The next day, Ella and Jordan were assigned to deep-clean the kitchen with Mr. Bridle.

"Hey," Jordan said to Ella as they entered the kitchen, equipped with matching rubber gloves. "I've been thinking about your . . . practice issue. Maybe you can talk to Mr. Bridle about it, like Madison said."

"Talk to me about what?" Mr. Bridle said, getting up from the floor. He had a bucket of dirty, soapy water in one hand and a huge sponge in the other. The knees of his jeans were soaked through.

"Ella wants to spend her free time practicing barrels," said Jordan. "But Madison told her no."

"As well she should. You all haven't been riding

long enough to be left unsupervised, and we older folks have things we have to do in the afternoons. That's why we give you free time. It means 'off time' for us." He winked at them, then realized Ella wasn't in the best mood about getting turned down, and cleared his throat. "Well . . . what if you supervised her, Jordan?"

Jordan's face drained of all color.

"What?" she squeaked.

"What?" said Ella. But Jordan was the same age as Ella! What business did she have supervising another kid? Teacher, sure. Overseer? No way.

"Sure." Mr. Bridle squeezed out his sponge into the dirty bucket and dug two more out of the cupboard under the sink. He handed one to each of them. "Why not? Jordan's been riding for years. I've seen you out in the arena, little lady. You have what it takes to handle the situation if anything goes wrong."

"N-n-no, I don't," said Jordan, backing away from them both like they'd come down with a highly contagious disease.

"Sure, you do," said Mr. Bridle gently. Jordan was about to object again, so Mr. Bridle said, "How about this, Jordan? I'll let you out of your chores for the week if you can supervise Ella during her extra horse work."

Jordan frowned. "But I like doing my chores. Gathering the eggs and milking the goats, at least."

He rubbed his chin. "Hmm. I didn't anticipate that."

This was Ella's chance. Her only chance. "Please, Jordan? Pretty, pretty please? I'll make your bed every morning."

"Every single morning?" said Jordan hopefully. Ella nodded. "I don't know . . ."

"And I'll take your plate to the sink after every meal."

"Whoa," said Mr. Bridle. "The stakes get higher."

"Every meal?" asked Jordan.

"Every single meal," said Ella.

Jordan swallowed, looked between Mr. Bridle and Ella, and gave a slow, reluctant nod. "Okay, fine. I'll do it. But I still want to do my chores. The others will get mad if they see I get to play around while they're all working."

Mr. Bridle stared at her, then laughed. "Okay. Sure. If you want, you can still do your chores."

Ella just shook her head. Jordan was still beyond her understanding. But Ella offered a big smile and said, "Thanks, man."

"All right, enough talking. More scrubbing." Mr. Bridle let out a sigh that didn't sound all too thrilled about getting stuck with this job, either. He pushed the bucket of water toward them. "Ella, you're on that end of the kitchen. Jordan, you're taking the pantry. We get through this early and I'll sneak us each a piece of pie from the fridge."

"Pie!" said Ella and Jordan together.

As they got to work, a thrill ran down Ella's spine. She was going to learn the barrels!

\\\

The moment they were in the arena the next afternoon, Figure Eight wanted to go, go, go—just like Ella did. Then she thought of the way her dad drove, always needing to get there *right now!* The way he blew through intersections, too impatient to stop, terrified her.

So Ella decided she was going to take it the way Mr. Bridle had forced her to with Lacey: slow and steady, to make sure she did it right this time.

Eight refused to walk along the rail as they warmed up, playing the same game—drifting toward the middle, cutting corners. Then, after the first two laps, she wouldn't stay at a walk and kept breaking into a trot. When Ella corrected her, Eight threw her ears back irritably, and sometimes simply ignored her.

What was Ella doing wrong? Each time Eight misbehaved, Ella jerked the reins back toward the rail and kicked harder, and harder, with her inside leg. But it seemed the harder she kicked, the less Eight listened.

Jordan didn't speak as Eight and Ella worked. At first, Ella liked it; this wasn't Madison, shouting instructions at her constantly from the center of the ring. But when Ella couldn't get Eight to listen, correction after correction, she grew irritated. She wanted Jordan to say something, to give her some kind of advice.

"What am I doing wrong?" Ella finally asked, yanking Eight to a stop near the railing where Jordan was standing.

"Um." Jordan scratched her head. "You're correcting only when she's totally out of sync—and you're pulling on her really hard. She's probably as frustrated as you are. Wouldn't it be annoying if you were screamed at for doing something wrong, but only long after you had started doing it?

Wouldn't you wish someone had told you sooner, more gently?"

Ella nodded slowly. Was that what she was doing to Figure Eight? She remembered what Fletch and Mr. Bridle had said about "yelling." Heat crept up Ella's neck. Had she been yelling at Eight this whole time without realizing it?

"You have to correct the moment you feel her start to come off the rail—like in that lesson we had with Mr. Bridle. Remember how when you felt Lacey start to speed up, you reminded her you were there and that you didn't approve of the gait change? She knew that you were paying attention and she immediately slowed down."

Jordan had been watching what Ella was doing?

"Yeah . . . I remember."

"Same thing. When you feel Eight start to come off the rail, just give her a gentle reminder that you're watching. And then if she continues to ignore you, correct her more severely."

Digesting this, Ella took Eight back at a trot. Within half a lap, Eight turned her head slightly toward the middle of the arena and began drifting.

"Correct now," called Jordan. "Just a whisper."

Ella gave a gentle tug on the rein, matching the

slight amount Eight was diverging from the path. She felt that connection again—that invisible line of tension between her hand and Figure Eight's mouth—and immediately, Eight answered, drifting back to the rail.

But there came no praise from Jordan, the way it would have come from Madison. Ella clenched the reins. She was going to have to do a lot better if she wanted applause.

"Remember to look where you want to go," said Jordan as they continued on around the arena, Eight still occasionally testing Ella, and Ella giving the same gentle corrective tug in response. "That will help her stay on the rail. Keep your eyes on the place you want to go, out toward the edge of the arena, and she'll follow. Look in the middle of the arena, and that's where she'll drift."

Soon Ella asked for a canter. Ella's eyes remained on the post just ahead of them, and Eight stuck to the outside of the arena like she had glue on her side.

"Awesome," Jordan called, giving a double thumbs-up. "But wrong lead."

"Lead?"

"She started cantering with the wrong front leg. Slow her to a trot and try again, and when you ask for the canter, do it just before the turn—that will help her take the right lead."

Ella restarted the canter a few times before Jordan said, "Yeah, that's it." And Ella could feel what she meant: the rhythm of the canter felt right, more balanced, on the correct lead. She'd never thought that much about the way a horse's legs moved.

After they were done warming up, Jordan ran out into the arena and set up the barrels without Ella saying a word. Once they were all arranged in a triangle shape, she scampered back out again. Ella trotted Eight through the pattern once, then twice.

"Looking good," Jordan said.

"That's all?" said Ella. She'd done at least three things wrong, she thought.

"Well . . ." Jordan climbed up onto the fence and sat on top of it. "You're just reining. But to get those really tight turns, you'll have to use your whole leg. Thigh, knee, heel."

"I don't know how to do that."

Jordan opened her mouth to speak, and then closed it again. She hopped down from the fence. "Here, stop real quick."

Ella slowed Eight to a halt and Jordan walked over, patting Eight's neck.

"When you're going around that first barrel— it's a right turn—you want to bend her around the barrel with your legs," Jordan said. "Why don't you start with your outside leg? Just move your knee forward." She took Ella's knee in one hand and set it forward on the horse. "Apply a little pressure just before you're ready to go around the barrel."

Jordan hopped out of the arena again as Ella took the barrel pattern a third time, still at a trot. Ella was so busy focusing on her knee that she didn't look where she was going. They were sailing past the barrel when she realized it was time to turn, and ended up jerking Eight's rein at the last moment. Figure Eight, surprised, flung her head toward the barrel and made an awkward loop.

Ella felt like there were just too many moving parts to track. But Jordan didn't say anything. Ella was the only one criticizing her own work.

On the second turn, Ella prepared. She looked where she wanted to go, and pressed in with her knee at the same time.

Eight bent perfectly around the barrel, and away from Ella's leg.

"Awesome," said Jordan. That was it. One word. Ella finished the barrels and waited for Jordan to say something else.

But she didn't. So Ella tried it again.

And again.

By the third try, her hands and her knee worked in perfect sync, and they cornered each of the barrels so closely that Ella even made one of them tip.

Jordan glanced at her watch. "I think we should go in," she said, and climbed down from the arena fence. "A few cool-down laps?"

She never gave orders, Ella realized—simply made requests, suggestions. It was nice. Ella always felt like she had a choice. Ella wondered if Jordan used that tactic with horses, too.

"Sure," said Ella. "And Jordan?"

Jordan paused before leaving the arena.

"Thank you."

She shrugged. "No problem," Jordan said. "Just doing what Mr. Bridle told me to do."

As Jordan walked away, Ella felt a twinge of disappointment. She wished Jordan *wanted* to be there, helping her, instead of simply doing it because Mr. Bridle told her to, or because Ella had bribed her.

But that was okay for now. Ella knew that the more she tried to force Jordan to be her friend, the more likely she'd push her away.

So she simply cooled down Figure Eight and then took her inside to brush her down.

\\\

Ma Etty was standing by the barn door when Ella approached with Eight.

"Looking really good out there," she said, and Ella wondered how long she'd been watching. "You're on your way to becoming the kind of horse-woman you'll need to be."

"For what?"

"For the amateur gymkhana show," Ma Etty said, grinning. "That's what."

"Gymkhana show . . . ?" asked Ella, not under-standing. And then, it hit her. "There's a show? Can I enter?" she asked, speaking so fast that the words almost didn't come out right. "Can I ride Figure Eight?"

"Sure," Ma Etty said, smiling smugly, as if she had anticipated this reaction. "If you work real hard, practice, and have lots of patience." She rubbed Figure Eight's big neck.

Ella couldn't believe this was happening.

"Yes!" she said. "Yes, I want to do it!"

"Great," Ma Etty said. "Willard will sign you up. It's in three weeks. And the first prize is a belt buckle! But you have to be on your best behavior, or you won't be going."

Ella nodded a dozen times. "Yes, yes! I will."

She put Eight away as quickly as she could and sprinted off to tell Jordan.

CHAPTER FIFTEEN

"**C**ool!" Jordan exclaimed when Ella told her about the show, during the tiny break they had before dinner to get cleaned up and changed. "So you get to be in a show." Jordan's eyes closed for a moment, like she was imagining the spectacle in her mind's eye. "And you get to show Figure Eight!"

"I know, right?" Ella sighed. "She's going to do so well out there." Ella hoped both of them would look awesome out in the arena, too, roaring around those barrels.

"It would be cool to go home with your own belt buckle," Jordan said.

"Heck yeah."

Ella was walking on clouds. Coasting on sunshine.

She wanted to hug Jordan, but didn't want to push her luck. So instead, as Ella took off her muddy riding boots and put on her sneakers, she said, "I'm going to have to learn how to go faster. Can't win barrels at a trot."

"Don't worry," Jordan said. "You're doing fine. I'm sure you won't have a problem getting to a gallop."

And sure enough, the next day Ella progressed from going at a fast trot around the barrels to taking them at a canter. She wanted to gallop so badly—to speed from barrel to barrel like those racers at the rodeo. But that was her instinct speaking. That was Dad, saying, *Go for it! Get what you want!*

For this, Ella needed to think like Jordan. If she wanted to do this right, she had to progress slowly, carefully. The understanding that Ella and Eight were forging only existed at the slower speeds so far. Ella could completely control Eight at a walk, a trot, and a canter around the barrels.

Galloping—that wild, speeding gait that she had only practiced along the rail—would require a different set of skills.

It was clear, though, that Eight wanted to run the

barrel pattern. She itched for it, jumping into faster gaits than Ella asked for as often as she could. Sometimes Ella let her sprint home from the last barrel, and Eight devoured it.

So, on their third lesson with Jordan, Ella decided to let her run.

"Any tips?" asked Ella, as she proposed her plan to Jordan.

"Don't fly off," she said, and climbed up to her usual spot on the arena fence to watch. "Hold onto your horn if you need to."

As Ella and Eight took off from one end of the arena toward the first barrel, Jordan shouted, "Woo hoo!" Then: "Remember to look!"

Ella's gaze locked onto a spot on the other side of the barrel. At first, her body flew up in the saddle, unused to the speed. But she adjusted her weight and settled deep in her seat, right on the pockets of her jeans, and flew right back down again.

As Eight approached the barrel, Ella pulled the reins to the side. With her legs she guided Eight around the barrel. Then they were clear of the first and it was on to the second, at full speed.

Ella dropped forward in the saddle, giving Eight

the reins, telling her she could finally go as fast as she wanted—as fast as she could.

Around the second barrel they flew. Ella guided Eight's big body around the turn, feeling the horse's muscles bunch up underneath her as she compressed her haunches and wrapped herself around the barrel—tight as a python strangling its prey.

Then, clear of the barrel, Eight extended again and exploded off the turn. They sprinted toward the last barrel.

Exhilaration filled Ella to the brim. The dirt sailed past beneath Eight's neck as the wind tossed Ella's braid. She hadn't known a horse could move this fast, hadn't imagined it even in her fantasies.

"Ella!" shouted Jordan. "Watch out!"

Ella snapped out of it to find that, rather than aiming for the spot just to the right of the third barrel, she'd guided Eight straight into it by staring at it.

Ella yanked the rein hard to one side. Eight veered, her head pulling against the sudden movement, but she didn't have enough time.

Eight's shoulder collided with the barrel. Then so did Ella's foot. Ella yelped in pain while Eight neighed in surprise, and they careened off to the side of the arena.

"Stop her!" called Jordan. "Ella! Whoa! Whoa!"

Jordan's urgent, steady voice drew Ella out of the panic. She pulled back hard on the reins as the far end of the arena loomed big and close—too close.

Eight slammed her hooves down into the dirt and came to an instant stop.

They both stood, breathing hard, for a tiny eternity. Jordan climbed down from the fence and jogged over to them. She patted Eight's sweaty neck, then Ella's sweaty leg.

"It's all right," she said, and Ella couldn't tell if she was speaking to her or the horse. Maybe to both of them. The panic that had overwhelmed her senses drained off, leaving Ella shaking and tearful.

Ella took a big gasp of air as the fear finally left her, leaving an aching chasm of disappointment.

"What did I do?" Ella asked, staring down at Eight's sweating neck. "What did I do wrong?"

"You didn't do anything wrong," Jordan said. She offered a hand up to Ella and Ella took it, letting Jordan help her down from the saddle. Jordan put an arm around her shoulders and squeezed.

Still holding onto Ella with one arm, Jordan checked the condition of Eight's shoulder where she had collided with the barrel.

"No harm done," Jordan said, showing the unmarred, doe-brown hair to Ella. "See?" Eight's velvety white nostrils flared with each deep breath, and her eyes were wide.

"I terrified her," said Ella, hiccuping with a sob that she held in. "I ruined her."

"You didn't ruin anything. You were both caught up in the moment." Jordan, one arm still wrapped around Ella's shoulders, took Eight's reins in her other hand and began walking the two of them around the arena to cool down. Silently they did one entire lap. Ella's breaths began to even out, and so did Eight's. The horse's great neck began to droop—stretching out, lowering to the ground.

"Look," said Jordan. "Everything's okay. Figure Eight's already relaxed again. She's not upset at you."

Ella glanced over. Eight looked so beautiful— her faded brown splotches, her white nose—and not injured at all. She probably had just been surprised by Ella's poor horsemanship.

"Jordan?" Ella asked.

"Yes?"

"Can . . . can you put Eight away for me?" Ella hated asking for the favor after causing this big mess, but she felt like an old statue slowly crumbling to bits. She couldn't bear to be around horses anymore today. She wanted to go sit down in the grass and cry alone for a while, until all the fear and frustration melted off her like a crust of ice in the sun.

"Of course," said Jordan. "No problem." Giving Ella one last squeeze, Jordan took Eight on another lap around the arena.

Ella jogged to the pasture, where she found a cool, grassy knoll overlooking the creek. She sat right at the top and watched the sun dip behind the mountains.

Why did Ella always screw up like this, right when things were starting to go right?

The tears that had been building up in the arena all tumbled out of her. She didn't even try to stop them.

Ella hadn't hurt Eight, and she hadn't been hurt herself. But if Ella got distracted again for even a second, the next time could be worse. What if it happened at the gymkhana show, in front of everyone? Jordan might not always be there.

If Eight got hurt, Ella would never, ever forgive herself.

\\\

Awhile later, someone padded up the hill behind Ella. Jordan sat down in the grass. For a long time, she didn't speak, and for once, Ella was fine with it. She didn't want to hear her own miserable voice anyway.

"You know," Jordan said after a while, "Eight gets excited whenever you come into the barn."

Ella glanced up, her face a crackly mask from crying. When she thought about it, Jordan was usually in the barn already when Ella showed up. Jordan observed things like that, things Ella didn't see. She was always paying attention.

"That horse loves to run," Jordan went on. "Don't think she ever got to run this much before you."

Sometimes the way Jordan talked about horses, it sounded like she was one. She seemed to understand them better than people.

"Why do you love horses so much?" Ella asked.

If the question surprised Jordan, she didn't show it.

She shrugged, her usual answer. Ella was going to leave it at that, but then Jordan said, "They're innocent. Pure. Like Eight—even though she seems a bit bratty, she's not. She just wants to run. Her desires are simple." She sighed. "I wish people were that simple."

"Huh." No one had ever spelled it out that way for Ella. People really were complicated. "How did you get into horseback riding?"

"It's the one thing that's mine," Jordan said. "And only mine."

That wasn't even close to an answer that Ella had expected. "You usually have to share?"

"I have five brothers and two sisters. I'm the third oldest."

Ella didn't know anyone who came from a family with eight kids.

"None of them ride?" she asked.

"We couldn't have a horse, even if my parents wanted one."

"Then how did you learn?"

"It found me. I was selling eggs to Mrs. Rose and I said something about her horses—she had three big, pretty quarter horses. I told her they were beautiful. She said, 'They are, aren't they? But I don't have time for them all.' Her husband had died and she had to take over his workload around the property. She didn't have enough time for the horses anymore and felt terrible about it.

"So after a while of me coming over and telling her how much I liked them, Mrs. Rose asked if I could help exercise them. She said she'd teach me how to ride in exchange for working them out a few times a week." It was the most Jordan had ever said at once. Ella wanted to keep her going.

"An initial investment for a long-term payoff," Ella said, repeating what her dad always said about why he worked so many long hours. This Mrs. Rose sounded like a clever lady. "That's really lucky for you. Free lessons!"

"Yep," said Jordan. "She taught me as much as she could and then she sent me out into the field. I ride three times a week and exercise all three horses. Mrs. Rose gives me a small lesson when she sees I need to learn something. For a while I had time to eat dinner with her before going home to do homework. But now, with Dad's gout, he can't walk much. Me and Olly had to pick up the slack—babysitting, helping with cooking, putting the kids to bed. So I just go over to Mrs. Rose's, ride them quick as I can, and run home."

The puzzle that was Jordan McAdam started to click together, forming a picture that Ella could finally make out. She was one girl out of eight kids, trying to help keep her family afloat.

"Is Olly your brother?" asked Ella.

"Older brother. My oldest sister's gone off to college, so Olly and I help out with the younger kids now while Mom works and takes care of Dad, since Dad can't work. Olly does even more around the house than I do so I can have my afternoons free for Mrs. Rose's horses." Jordan stared down at the open palms of her hands. "I try to do as much as I can to make up for it—make the kids breakfast, help them with their homework, wash Olly's clothes. But the best thing is to just be quiet, because noise upsets Dad."

Ella didn't know what to say. After a moment she asked Jordan, "Would you run the barrels tomorrow?"

"What?" asked Jordan.

"Ride Loco Roco through the barrel pattern so I can watch. I want to see how you do it."

"I don't know how I could show you anything helpful, Ella . . ."

Her enduring humility was almost annoying. "You know tons more than I do," said Ella. "You've already given me so many helpful tips. But now I want to see it in action. I want to observe you."

"Like I'm a science experiment?"

"Exactly! Just imagine I'm the mad scientist and you're the experiment. I want to watch you do your thing and take notes. Would you do that?"

Ella realized it was unfair of her to phrase it as a favor, after Jordan had spilled her guts. Jordan was the kind of person that wanted to help everyone, to fill all the gaps, and Ella already knew Jordan would agree.

"Yeah, I guess I can ride for you," Jordan said.

"Great. Tomorrow, then." Ella stood up, already feeling better, and stretched. "Thank you, by the way."

Jordan gave her a funny look. "For what?"

"For everything. For teaching me. For calming me down. For putting Eight away."

"I'm just doing what Mr. Bridle told me to do," Jordan said, as if gratitude was a foreign language she didn't understand.

This time, Ella smiled at that. The way Jordan had helped her back there—she wasn't doing this anymore just because Mr. Bridle told her. The barrels held the same power over her that they did over Ella.

"Thanks again," Ella said. And she meant it.

CHAPTER SIXTEEN

The next day, when they were done with their chores, Jordan and Ella met up at the barn. Jordan didn't speak as she tacked up Loco Roco. She did in five minutes what usually took Ella twenty. Tacking up, riding, and putting away two or three horses every afternoon? That would make Ella pretty fast at it, too.

Once on Loco's back, something in Jordan's demeanor shifted. She sat straight, but not stiff. Relaxed and poised at the same time, like she belonged there.

"It's all in here," Jordan told Ella, who was watching from Jordan's usual perch on top of the arena fence. Jordan patted her belly as she said it. "All good riding starts right here."

It was a mysterious way of putting it, but Ella knew what she meant. She'd felt that, too—how everything she did on her horse rotated around that center of gravity right in her abdomen.

Jordan started with a simple warm-up, walking Loco in patterns around the arena. Half the time, Ella couldn't even see the commands Jordan was giving— but after a while she could make out Jordan's thighs giving a squeeze, or her heel nudging his side, or her left elbow tucking just a little further in to put more pressure on the reins.

Jordan finished the warm-up with scientific precision. When she was done, Ella ran out to set up the barrels.

Without preamble, Jordan kicked Loco and they leapt into a gallop. Ella felt like she was at the rodeo again as Loco's legs flew, kicking up clouds of dust. Jordan had only been riding Loco for a few weeks, but already they seemed as close as Paul and his horse, Roy: speaking without words, listening to each other's thoughts. Loco turned so tightly around each barrel that the angle of his body tipped nearly parallel with the ground. Jordan's ponytail sailed behind her like a brown flag. Horse and girl moved in perfect synchronicity.

They came to the final barrel. Jordan sat forward in the saddle, lending her momentum to her horse. Her thighs and knees and heels all worked together as Loco whipped around the barrel so fast that Jordan had to hold onto the pommel of her saddle to avoid falling off. Loco's breath came in great gusts as he passed Ella and sprinted to the finish line.

Ella clapped as Loco slowed to a trot and made a loop on the opposite end of the arena. Jordan walked to where Ella sat on the fence. Loco was sweating.

"Was that helpful?" Jordan asked.

A mixture of feelings had overcome Ella. Why couldn't she ride like Jordan? She made it look so easy. But now, after the hours Ella had already put into it, she saw that it probably hadn't been.

Still—what an amazing thing to witness up close! Jordan and Loco were the real deal. And Ella was lucky.

"Yeah," she said. "It was incredibly helpful. Thank you, Jordan."

Jordan looked away. "I didn't do anything."

"You've done a ton. Look, you're spending your free time teaching me how to ride. That's a pretty big deal."

"Just paying forward what Mrs. Rose did for me. Anyway, I've already taught you everything I know. I told you it wasn't very much."

"You taught me so much already today," Ella said. Why couldn't Jordan give herself any credit? "Just watching you, I learned a ton."

"Oh." Jordan appeared stumped by this answer. "Well . . . okay. As long as it's helpful to you."

"Will you do it again?" asked Ella.

Jordan finally looked up. "Um, sure. Why not?" She turned back to the starting line. "Loco, let's go try that one more time. For Ella."

\\\

Half an hour before dinner, Jordan stopped her demonstration.

"Hey, Ell, want to tack up Eight and do a short ride for our cool-down? Even if she doesn't get a real big workout today, I bet she'd enjoy getting out."

"Oh yeah," said Ella, jumping off the fence. She went inside, tacked up Eight quickly, and mounted. She jogged out to meet Jordan at the gate leading out of the arena.

"Shoot," said Ella, shooting an accusing look at

the gate. "Should have stayed on the ground so I could open that."

"Got it," said Jordan.

She tapped Loco Roco's shoulder with her heel and tugged only his opposite rein toward the gate. He took a step sideways toward the fence, to avoid coming at it head-on, but Jordan was still too far away to reach the latch.

It was like watching the trick rider and her horse. Jordan clicked, repeated her request for a side step, and Loco sidled up to the gate. She reached over, plucked the latch open, and managed to hold onto the end of the gate while Loco walked through. With a subtle motion of her heel and her rein, Jordan pulled Loco around sideways so she could get out of the way and let Ella through. Once Eight had trotted out of the arena, Jordan pushed the gate closed behind them.

"Wow," said Ella. "That's a good trick."

"Not a trick, just closing a gate."

"But it looks hard!"

Jordan smiled. "It's not, I promise. Just use your legs the same way I've been showing you out in the ring." She patted Loco on the neck. "And think about what you want to accomplish. Remember what Mr.

Bridle said—your horse feels what you feel."

She made it sound like some kind of animal magic, but Ella didn't think it was quite that simple.

"Try it when we get back," said Jordan.

So after their short ride, Ella tried to position Eight by the gate, just so she could reach the latch. But Eight flung her head around, and kept turning side to side so Ella couldn't reach. Ella grew irritated that Eight wouldn't listen.

"It just takes time," said Jordan, climbing off Loco Roco and opening the gate by hand. "You're already almost there."

CHAPTER SEVENTEEN

Lessons during free time continued all that week, and the next. The show bore down on Ella like a squealing steam engine.

That Friday night, Ella took Jordan's dishes to the sink after dinner, as usual.

"Still at it, Jeeves?" Kim asked as Ella dumped her two piles into the sink. He poked fun at her for this every single night, but not in the poisonous way he used to. Ella liked having someone she could spar with.

"Still at it, until the day I wake up a barrel-racing prodigy," said Ella.

"Let me know when you figure that magic potion out."

When they re-entered the dining room, Ma

Etty was bringing out cinnamon rolls. They seemed full of meaning, or maybe it was the extra layer of frosting.

"You all have been so focused this week," said Ma Etty. "So we wanted to surprise you with something cool."

Ella perked up. What would the Bridles offer them that qualified for the word 'cool'? Whatever it was, Paul, who had joined them for dinner, was practically bouncing in his seat.

"Okay, tell them," Mr. Bridle said, giving a little eye roll.

"We're going on a trail ride!" Paul said, obviously thrilled.

Ella didn't know whether to be ecstatic or worried. The last trail ride had been disastrous. She and Jordan exchanged a look.

"What about practice?" Ella whispered.

"It's okay," said Jordan. "A day off would be good for Eight. Horses need them, just like people do."

"All three of us are taking you," Paul went on, managing to sling a single arm over both Madison and Fletch. He gave them a comrade's squeeze. "We'll stop at the lake and make a picnic out of it, maybe do some fishing?"

"Fishing!" Drew's hair seemed to stand up straighter. "If we catch something, can we cook it for dinner? Please?"

Ma Etty raised both eyebrows. "Sure. Why not?"

"Blech," Jordan whispered to Ella. "Fish!"

"Not a fan?"

"Not in your lifetime. Tastes like . . . fish."

Ella preferred this version of Jordan—the funny, sometimes downright talkative Jordan that had started making the occasional appearance. Ella didn't know if that Jordan had always been there, or if the two of them were rubbing off on each other. Maybe, Ella thought, it was Loco Roco's influence.

They feel what you feel. Could it go the other way around, too?

She had thoughts like this all the time now, thoughts that sounded like Jordan or Mr. Bridle—or even her mom—was speaking.

"Great," said Paul. "Tomorrow morning, nine o'clock sharp, meet me outside the barn with horses saddled and ready." He turned to his plate to start tearing into his cinnamon roll. Then he stopped and said, "But no risky business!"

"Aw," Ash said to Kim, with his lower lip protruding. "There go our nefarious business plans."

"But, Dallas," groaned Kim, "what about my secret lair? I was promised a secret lair."

"Don't worry. We'll build it out of the bones of our enemies if we have to."

"No bone lairs, either!" said Paul.

\\

"So you're telling me the Falcons are going to not only beat the Cowboys this year," said Ash, turning halfway around in his saddle, "but will make it to the Super Bowl? You realize it's been years since the Falcs even got close, right?"

"Yeah, but we have this new guy this year." Drew raised two fingers to his chest. "Trust me. It's going to happen. Your beloved Cowboys are going down."

"The Falcons are losers."

Drew opened his mouth to say something, but their argument had agitated his horse. "Whatever, man," he said, slowing down so he fell in line next to Ella, instead of Ash.

"Wouldn't be unheard of for the Falcons to beat the Cowboys," said Fletch. "Those mid-list teams always make a comeback eventually."

Ash was about to reply, but Ella broke in. "Could

we please talk about something besides football? My eardrums are melting."

Jordan raised her hand. "I second that motion. Dogs, maybe? Like, how cute are these three goofballs?"

The dogs chased one another in circles in the woods, running back occasionally to make sure they hadn't lost their master, then taking off again.

"Actually," said Paul, "the big surprise is coming up." He pointed off in the direction of the distant tree line.

"Aren't we almost to Cougar Point?" asked Madison.

"Cougar . . . Point?" asked Kim, his voice faltering a bit at the end. "Why is it called that?"

Madison laughed. "Why do you think? This place used to be overrun with cougars." Kim's eyes widened and he wrapped one hand around the pommel of his saddle, like it would save him from a cougar attack. "But that was a hundred years ago. The sheriff put a bounty out on cougars decades ago because they were killing sheep, and the hunters went wild. Not many cougars left now."

"That's sad," said Jordan. "They're just trying to live. It's their role in the ecosystem to eat other animals."

Ella marveled that Jordan could feel so much sympathy for cat-shaped killing machines.

"I'd put a bounty on any animal that could end me with one paw swipe." Kim batted at the air with one hand. "Forget it."

Jordan pressed her lips together and didn't speak, but Ella could practically hear the diatribe she was biting back. The other night, Jordan had found a spider crawling on her pillow and screamed. Instead of killing it, she urged it onto a paper towel and sprinted outside, where she set it down in the grass.

"Why bother?" Ella had asked.

"They eat bugs," she said. "Mosquitos and stuff. Without them, the mosquitos would take over. Just trying to maintain the balance."

They crested a ridge and from the front Paul said, "Guess you're right, Maddie. We've reached Cougar Point. Look."

A valley swept out below them. A lake, clear and still as a mirror, had carved out a bowl in the valley basin. Their mouths hung open as they took in the view.

"And that is the glacial lake we missed last time," said Paul.

"I guess I'll be okay fishing there," Drew said.

As they headed down the mountainside, Fletch told them, "Lean back! Center of gravity!" Figure Eight's feet expertly picked a path down the steep slope. The drop-off on the other side made Ella's heart race, but the horses seemed to know exactly what they were doing.

Half an hour later, everyone arrived safely at the base of the hill. Paul tied the animals nearby while the kids helped Fletch and Madison unpack the food and the blankets. Then they stripped to their swimsuits and leapt in the lake.

"Hey!" hollered Drew, just sitting down with the fishing line he'd rigged up. "Stop scaring away my fish!"

But they got out quickly because the water was ice cold, and only Fletch seemed immune to it. Ella and Jordan dried off and pulled out their lunches, joining Madison on a blanket.

"How's barrel racing camp been going?" Madison asked Ella and Jordan. "You two missing your free time yet?"

"What free time?" asked Jordan. "I don't know what that is."

"Pfft," said Ella. "Not like you did anything cool with it before. You were always moping."

"Yeah, but now when will I get my moping in?" asked Jordan.

Ella laughed. "I carved out a slot for you in the schedule right after dinner."

"Great. Now you want me to mope and brush my teeth at the same time? What do you think I am, your trick pony?"

Madison rolled her eyes. "Okay, okay. So you're having fun, I take it. Think you'll be ready by next week?"

"Of course," Ella said, folding her arms. Wow. She sounded like her dad. Probably looked like him just then, too, arms crossed over his chest as he said, "Of course." Like you'd just asked him the most obvious question possible.

Madison laughed. "Okay. Good. Not that I had any doubt, of course. The two of you must make a killer team." She snorted a little. "Like Jekyll and Hyde."

"Hey!" Ella said. "Does that make me Hyde?"

"I'm too tall to be Ella's Jekyll," said Jordan. "And Jekyll and Hyde are the same guy, right? They couldn't exist at the same time."

"Well, uh, yeah," said Madison, caught off guard. "But one was the scientist, you know . . . The other one was the monster." She shook her head. "Okay, bad analogy."

"No, no." Ella snickered. "That's accurate. Jordan's the brain, I'm the maniac."

\\

As Ella watched Ash, Fletch, and Madison throwing a Frisbee, and Paul showing Drew how to cast the fishing line, she had the unwelcome thought that days like this were limited.

"Only ten more days of camp," Ella said to Jordan, passing back the apple they were sharing. She sighed. "I don't want to go back to Petaluma."

Jordan raised both eyebrows as she bit into the apple. "Really?" she said, a little food in her mouth. "I can't wait. I've really missed Olly and Lola and the others."

"I guess I wouldn't know," said Ella. "No siblings."

"None? Not even step-siblings?"

Ella shook her head. "Maybe my dad will remarry," she said. She'd come to terms with this eventuality when Dad started dating again. That she might have a step-mom someday. Step-siblings. Half-siblings.

"What about your mom?" asked Jordan.

Ella shrugged. "Dunno. We don't talk."

"Oh."

Ella could tell Jordan wanted to ask why, but she probably didn't want to seem nosy.

"We don't really get along," Ella said, but as soon as it came out of her mouth, she wondered if what she really meant was, *She and my dad don't get along*. Ella hadn't seen her mom in almost two years, making up reasons why she couldn't visit. She had no idea if they'd see eye-to-eye at all anymore. During the divorce proceedings, the judge had determined both of Ella's parents fit for custody—but with her mom moving across the country, they had left it up to Ella to decide where to spend the majority of her time.

Of course she'd thrown her chips in with Dad. He was staying put in their old house; he understood her the way Mom couldn't.

Or, at least, she'd thought so.

"I'm sorry," Jordan said.

Ella batted a hand at her. "Whatever. I'm not hung up on it." But she had started thinking about Mom a lot more since she'd been at the ranch. Especially since she'd become friends with Jordan.

The sure way in which she thought about being

friends with Jordan took Ella by surprise. When had that happened?

Jordan didn't say anything else, and Ella supposed her flippancy hadn't been encouraging, either. So Ella said, "Jordan, can I ask you a personal question?"

Jordan turned her head away, and Ella was worried she was drawing into herself again—but she returned a second later with another apple.

"Ask away," Jordan said.

"Why are you even here?" asked Ella. "You're like . . . the least troublesome person I bet they've ever had at Quartz Creek Ranch."

Jordan laughed. "I doubt it. What did Ma Etty say, that they've been doing this for twenty years?"

"Come on, Jordan."

The smile fell off Jordan's lips. She searched Ella's face, as if she expected to find that Ella was joking—that she didn't actually expect an answer to her question. When Jordan seemed to realize that Ella was perfectly serious, she sighed.

"Grades."

Then she took another bite of her apple and stared at her feet.

"Like, you failed a class?" said Ella.

"*Like*," said Jordan, mocking Ella's tone, "I failed all my classes."

There was a long pause. Ella waited, thinking Jordan would give her more. But she didn't.

"Why?" Ella asked. "Did you get sick?"

Another long pause.

"Why not?" Jordan asked, surprisingly forceful and a little angry. "Why try? Trying is a waste of time when you know you're going to fail."

"Each year is a chance to start over," Ella said. "You don't know for sure you're going to fail."

"No," snapped Jordan. "I do know." She looked Ella right in the eyes as she said, "Every time I try, I fail. I've worked and worked in school but even my best isn't enough. So why bother?" She stood up and threw her apple core. Ella, perplexed, watched it roll away. Jordan had given her a hard time the other day just for tossing a strawberry head.

"You've succeeded at lots of things, Jordan," Ella said. "You're the best horseback rider I know."

"My folks thought that, too. They sent me here hoping it would magically make me good at every-thing." She narrowed her eyes. "As if spending half a summer riding horses would turn me into somebody like you—somebody who believes totally and blindly in themselves. But I'm not. And I'm not the rider you think I am."

Ella ignored the insult. "Yes, you are!" She wanted to yell it at Jordan but she knew it would only scare her. "I think you're great," Ella said, feeling heat work its way up into her throat. But it wasn't anger—not like usual. She was sad, frustrated, that Jordan was acting so obtuse. "Does what I think not matter at all to you?"

"You don't know anything about riding, Ella."

It hit Ella like a kick to the rib cage.

"So how would you know it if you saw it?" Jordan went on. "Psh, 'the best horseback rider.' What do you know?" Jordan turned away. "Nothing, that's what. So stop pretending you do. I'm going for a swim."

Sticking her hands in her pockets, Jordan walked away, leaving Ella alone on the picnic blanket.

Ella stood up.

"You're . . . you're . . ." Ella couldn't think of anything better to say, so she shouted after her, "You're a jerk for saying that, Jordan!"

But Jordan didn't answer from down the hill. Paul and Drew looked up, probably wondering what she was yelling about.

Ella sat back down, wanting to strangle someone.

She hastily wiped at tears forming in her eyes and steeled herself against them. She wasn't going to give Jordan the benefit of crying.

Ella hadn't thought that quiet, shy girl had it in her to be cruel like that. It hurt worse than being punched.

So maybe Jordan was right and Ella didn't know much about horsemanship. She could cop to that. But Ella had seen Jordan ride. She'd heard about the regional championship. The Bridles trusted her.

How could Jordan think so little of herself?

CHAPTER EIGHTEEN

Jordan didn't speak at all on the ride home, and when the other kids occasionally asked her things, she responded with *yes*, *no*, or a shrug. Ella hoped Jordan would be out of her funk by tomorrow, when they needed to resume training for the show the next weekend. They couldn't afford to lose even a single day.

Ella still had a lot to do before she was ready to perform in front of a judge.

\\

But Jordan didn't speak to Ella at all during the daily lesson with Fletch and Madison. Then, after chores, it was time for practice.

Jordan wasn't in the barn waiting when Ella arrived, so she tacked up Eight and went out to warm up while she waited. But ten minutes later, Jordan still hadn't appeared.

Ella couldn't waste time waiting, so she decided to get on with her practice. She took Eight around the barrels at a canter, but felt nervous going whole hog without Jordan there.

And what if someone caught Ella working out here alone? She couldn't afford to mess up before the show and risk Mr. Bridle changing his mind about letting her go.

Ella walked Eight up to the gate leading out of the arena. She didn't want to waste time getting off and on the horse. She remembered Jordan and Loco Roco opening the gate together, and decided to ask Eight to sidle up to it.

Eight was coming in at a direct angle, though, and Ella was too far away.

She thought about it for a moment. Her lesson with Jordan returned to her.

Ella pressed in with the heel opposite the gate, keeping Eight's head positioned straight ahead. *I want to open the gate*, she thought, directing her gaze at the latch she wanted to reach. *Let's open the gate together and go on a nice long ride.*

Eight immediately stepped sideways, lining up with the gate. Ella reached over and lifted the latch, letting the gate swing open beside them. Then she walked Eight through the open doorway, using opposite leg and rein to spin her around. Ella had to get Eight even closer on the other side so she could reach the open gate and pull it closed again.

When she finished, Ella glanced up automatically to look for the approval on Jordan's face. But she wasn't there.

Ella wandered the ranch, looking for signs of her absent teacher. Kim and Drew were playing bean bag toss.

"Whoa, hey, Ella," said Drew, dropping the bean bags when he saw her ride up on Eight. "What are you doing out here?"

"Seen Jordan?" she asked.

"Not since lunch."

"I had chores with her," said Kim. "She left right after. What are you doing riding around on this side of the ranch alone? Won't you get in trouble?"

Shoot. Ella hadn't thought about that. She'd been on a mission to find Jordan and thought this was the fastest way to do it.

Ella dismounted and led Figure Eight back to the barn before any of the trainers saw her. Inside, she found Loco Roco's stall empty.

Silent and stealthy. Jordan must have come as soon as Ella left to go find her.

Ella exhaled and glanced at Figure Eight. The horse nudged her, hoping for a treat. Ella dug one out of her pocket and handed over the goods. Where had Jordan gone?

Trying is a waste of time when you know you're going to fail.

You don't know anything about riding, Ella.

Maybe Jordan looked at Ella as a venture. As something she had tried. Teach that loud, angry girl how to talk quietly to her horse.

Maybe Ella had failed, so Jordan had given up.

"Well," Ella said aloud to Eight, "I haven't failed *me* yet. I'm still signed up for the show."

She had to trust herself if she was going to take the barrels at full tilt. She had to be careful. Back out in the arena, Ella set up the barrels alone, then climbed on Eight's back.

Figure Eight knew what was coming as soon as they reached the starting line, and broke into a nervous trot. Ella took a deep breath and sat deep in her saddle.

She tested the reins, and felt Eight respond to them. Gentle reminders to slow down brought Eight back to a walk. Another deep, relaxing breath. The barrels didn't exist yet. Ella kept her eyes on the barn, away from the barrels.

Eight's neck drooped as she relaxed. She was ready.

Ella looped them around to face the three barrels, off on the other side of the arena. Then, she leaned forward, and kicked.

Eight leapt into motion.

She galloped toward the first barrel. Ella kept her eyes on the spot behind it, where she wanted Eight to go, and indicated with her heel and just a bit of rein. She wanted to turn soon. Eight leaned her head in.

She had heard.

Just before the barrel, Eight's body curved. They spun around the first barrel and whipped on to the second.

Nothing slipped through Ella's mind except: *Look. Heel. Rein. Body.* She helped Eight around each turn with her own weight, using her thighs to keep them in sync.

Then they were clear of the second barrel and cannonballing toward the third. Eight's breaths went *huf huf huf* in time with the beat of her hooves.

Ella gazed past the next barrel and Eight slowed, just enough for Ella to push her around it. Ella felt the barrel graze the tip of her boot.

Then they were clear of the last barrel.

Facing the final length of the race, wind hurling her braid all around her neck, Ella leaned forward and let Eight have the reins. Figure Eight leapt forward, toward home, hurling dust into the air as they raced to the finish line.

Reaching the other end of the arena, Ella slowed Eight to a trot. As they started a cool-down lap, someone clapped.

"Looking good," said Mr. Bridle. He leaned against the fence and glanced around. "But where's Jordan?"

Ella shrugged. "She didn't show up today."

He rubbed his chin. She hoped he wouldn't chew her out for being here alone.

"Should have told someone," he said.

"I'm sorry. I just have so little time left to prepare for the show, I didn't want to waste it."

Mr. Bridle nodded. "It's done," he said. "No use dwelling on it. But I wonder what happened. Did you two have a fight?"

"I guess. But it wasn't my fault. I didn't lose my temper."

"That's good. I'm sure she'll come back when she's ready."

"Everyone says that." Ella walked Eight away from the fence and did a figure eight. "But I need her now."

"I don't think so. You looked pretty good out there." Mr. Bridle stood up straight and tipped his hat. "I think all that needs is some spit and polish, and you're ready."

"Whoa," Ella said to Eight, just sitting up in her seat a little to earn a halt. "You think so, Mr. Bridle?"

"Of course I do. I wouldn't say it if I didn't. Jordan's been a great teacher."

"I know!" Ella urged Eight back into a walk to work off the sweat. "I tried to tell her that, too, but she wouldn't believe me. She said I didn't know enough about horses to know the difference."

Mr. Bridle's eyebrows went up. "Our Jordan said that?"

Ella nodded.

"Well, from what I saw, she's doing something," said Mr. Bridle. "Still has a lot to learn, but don't we all? I've been teaching people how to know and ride horses for half my life and I'm always learning new stuff."

"Jordan doesn't see it that way. I think I failed her."

"I'm sure that's not true."

But Mr. Bridle didn't know Jordan.

"Well," said Mr. Bridle, "I guess I better come out and watch you if Jordan's falling down in her duties. You still have a show to prepare for."

That's right—the show! An idea occurred to Ella.

Maybe she could prove to Jordan that she hadn't failed . . . by winning that first-prize belt buckle.

\\

On Thursday, they were all told they'd be going on a field trip to the gymkhana show to cheer Ella on. The other kids wanted to know how training was going.

"Minus a teacher," Ella said, looking at Jordan as she said it, "but just drilling exercises with Mr. Bridle. One day at a time." She'd stopped taking Jordan's plates to the sink and making her bed. Now Jordan took her plates herself, and the bed sat unmade all day, to Madison's annoyance.

"Hard core," said Kim. "Figure Eight's gonna be great."

"If anybody can kick butt at this, it's you, Ella," said Drew.

It was sweet of them to encourage her, but she wished Jordan would say something, instead of just pick at her food. Ella missed her friend—goofing around, talking about horses. This silent war sucked.

Before Ella knew it, Friday rolled around: her last day before the show. Madison came into the barn just as Ella was tacking up and said, "Take the day off."

Ella remembered what Jordan had told her about horses needing a day off, too.

"We will be working pretty hard tomorrow," Ella said, lowering the blanket she was about to put on. "Maybe we should just walk around today, huh, Eight?"

"Go take Figure Eight and see if Paul needs help with something," said Madison. "Spend some time with her meditating about your future victory."

Pleased that Madison was allowing her to ride alone, Ella finished tacking up and mounted outside. She headed north along Bridlemile Road, where Paul and his ranch hands did their work, secretly hoping she'd run into Jordan.

She wanted to be mad. Her teacher had abandoned her just a few days before the big event. But more than anything, she just wanted things to go back to the way they were.

As Ella and Eight padded through the pasture, following the creek, Ella spotted a dark shape sitting up in a tree. A tan horse stood underneath it, drinking out of the creek. It was Loco Roco.

Up in the tree, Jordan ignored Ella's approach and kept staring up at the sky.

"Jordan?" asked Ella, flabbergasted. So this was where she'd been. "This is what you're doing with your free time now?"

Jordan shrugged, not saying anything.

"Great," said Ella. "First you're mean to me. Then you abandon me at practice. Now you're going to pretend like I don't exist?" She reined Eight around. "Fine. I don't need any of your mopey self-loathing anyway."

"First, you're going to pretend like I don't exist," said Jordan, mocking Ella's tone again. "Then you're going to be mean to me. Now you're going to call me a liar and then expect me to be your friend?"

Okay, so maybe Ella did call her that one time. "I'm sorry I said that," she said. "But it was . . . before, you know?" Before what, Ella wasn't exactly sure. Before she decided to stop being a jerk to everyone?

"Whatever." Jordan leaned back in the tree. Ella waited for her to say something else, but Jordan just plucked leaves off a branch and tossed them to the ground.

"Urgh!" Ella said. "You're so irritating!"

Ella backed away from Jordan and Loco Roco, turned Figure Eight around, and urged her up out of the creek bed. She wanted to knock Jordan's lights out. Maybe that's what it would take to wake her up.

No, Ella thought. Jordan would come around on Saturday. With that first-place ribbon hanging off Figure Eight's saddle, and the buckle clipped onto her belt—then Jordan would see.

CHAPTER NINETEEN

Saturday morning, anticipation got Ella up earlier than Jordan or even the sun. She found Eight in the barn and took her outside, tying her up by the pasture with a bucket of grain and standing with her as she ate.

Paul pulled the trailer around and they loaded up. The two of them drove to the fairgrounds alone; Fletch, Madison, the Bridles, and the other kids would join them later.

First, they registered and parked among the assorted cars and trailers. This was much smaller than the rodeo, but even this early in the morning, the place buzzed with activity. It was a youth show, so she wouldn't race against adults. But some of the kids she saw warming up looked like they'd grown up in the saddle.

Paul offered Ella a cowboy hat. "Here. This will help you blend in, city kid."

They unloaded Figure Eight and gave her something to eat as they relaxed, getting accustomed together to a new environment. Then it was time to tack up and start warming up.

The morning was hot and full by the time the white Quartz Creek Ranch van appeared. The kids piled out and checked out the surroundings, but Ella was focused on what she had to do.

It was time to win.

\\

There were twenty-one contestants in Ella's group.

Ella glanced around at the other people waiting. Some her own age, some younger, most of them older. A serious-looking boy in a nice hat rode a big bay quarter horse. A tall girl sat on a small Arabian who obeyed her every command. They all warmed up with expert hands.

"Hey, tiger," Drew said to Ella, patting Figure

Eight on the neck as he, Kim, and Ash wandered over. "You're gonna do great."

"Never said I wouldn't," said Ella.

Ash barked a laugh. "That's Ella, always confident. Hey, have you seen Jordan at all?"

Ella slowly shook her head. She'd been looking, but Jordan had turned invisible. "No, I haven't."

"Hmm. She took off right when we got here. Haven't seen her since."

"Whatever," said Kim. "You've got to focus on winning that prize, Ell. What was it, a gift certificate or something?"

"A belt buckle," said Ella. "One of those big ones."

"Oooh," said Kim, laughing. "I'd prefer the gift certificate."

"I think belt buckles are sweet," said Drew. "It's something you can't just buy. It's special. Anyway, good luck! I hope you win."

"Thanks, Drew." Ella rolled her eyes at the other two. "Can't just root for me, can you?"

Kim made a *woo woo* noise. "I'll root for you to win a gift certificate."

Ella wasn't really listening to them. She was watching the other contestants. The guy with the nice hat was up. He led his massive quarter horse into the arena, and it pawed at the ground as they waited to start.

It was like being at the rodeo again, watching him tear around each barrel and hurtle through each curve at enviable velocity. The time had barely started counting down when he'd completed the pattern and was thundering home again.

The crowd roared.

"Twenty-two point one seconds!" said the announcer.

As the guy with the nice hat, now minus the hat, led his bay out of the arena, the announcer called, "In the hull is Ella Pierson!"

Two more people ahead of her. Ella's pulse leapt to full throttle and Eight threw her head up. Ella could tell the horse felt her excitement. Eight already wanted to head toward the arena.

"Not our turn yet," Ella told the horse.

"Come on, everyone," said Ma Etty, appearing with food and drinks, Mr. Bridle at her side. "Let's leave Ella and Eight alone to get ready."

"Good luck," said Ash, waving, and the kids left to get good seats.

"You'll do great out there," Ma Etty said, walking away. "Don't worry!"

But Ella wasn't worrying about out there—she was worrying about right here. Eight wouldn't stop dancing, yanking on the reins, wanting to be out in the arena and running already. No matter how much Ella tried, she couldn't calm Eight down.

Paul strode over, eating a hot dog. "It's your nerves," he said. "I bet she's responding to your anxiety."

"My anxiety? What anxiety?" Ella demanded, and her voice cracked. Eight tossed her head back. "Okay. Maybe I see what you mean."

She wished Jordan were here. Jordan always knew what to say to calm her down.

"Hey, hey," said Paul, rubbing Eight's neck with one hand as the horse hopped from one foot to the other. "Settle down, girl."

"On deck," said the loudspeaker, "is Ella Pierson!"

The contestant out in the ring galloped back to the finish line and the announcer called out, "And Juniper Crowley goes home with twenty-one point eight seconds!"

The next contestant, a round guy on a draft pony who had been standing patiently in the starting pen, entered the ring. Next was Ella's turn.

As she approached the gate to the starting pen,

Eight flung her head to the side, ready to jump into the arena and run the race. Ella had never seen her like this. The more Eight slipped out of her control, the more Ella grew afraid. She knew the basic rules: if your horse couldn't stay under your control on the way into the starting area, they wouldn't let you race.

Paul took Eight by the reins and led her to the gate.

"Ella Pierson?" asked the attendant.

"That's me." Figure Eight tried to pull away from Paul and danced sideways.

"Calm that horse down," the attendant said. "Or I can't let you in."

Ella couldn't get Eight to slow down to a walk, no matter how many times she gently corrected her. Her nerves wouldn't settle, and Eight knew it.

"Sorry," said the attendant, making a check on his sheet. "Too risky."

"Too risky?" asked Paul. "The horse is just a little excited to race, that's all."

The attendant eyed them. Time was ticking— the contestant currently in the ring was almost done. Ella was up next. She tried to relax, as Madison had once told her. While Paul tried unsuccessfully to calm down Figure Eight, Ella remembered opening the arena gate back at the ranch.

We're back at the ranch, Ella thought, closing her eyes. *It's just us and the barrels.*

Ella tried to recall that feeling—the gentle calm they shared before Ella gave the cue. She needed that focus now.

Gently, Ella tested the connection in the reins.

She sat deep in her saddle seat.

She thought only about the race. She looked where she wanted to go—inside the starting area. She thought only of her goal—to win. She let her shoulders relax.

Eight's breathing slowed and her neck dropped. While Paul debated with the attendant, Ella and Eight calmly walked past them, into the starting pen, just as the previous contestant exited.

"Guess they're ready," said Paul, closing the gate behind them.

"Next contestant is in," the attendant said into his walkie-talkie.

"And Jack Lipman walks away with twenty-two point one seconds!" roared the announcer.

Ella and Eight faced the starting gate.

Eight didn't paw. She didn't dance. Ella and Eight

stared ahead at the barrels and for a moment, Ella thought she could hear what Eight was thinking. How she was seeing the pattern ahead of them as a series of timings, of curves, of twists and sprints.

The gate opened.

Eight stepped into the arena. Around them, the sky and the people and the announcer's voice vanished, and all that was left were those three white metal barrels, arranged in a triangle.

The attendant gestured at her. "Go!" he mouthed. "Your turn!"

Ella stared straight ahead at the first barrel. Then she leaned forward in the saddle, let Eight have the reins, and kicked.

Eight sprang into a gallop. She roared toward the first barrel, perfectly following Ella's line of sight.

Look.

Ella let her gaze wrap around the barrel.

Feet.

She guided the front of Eight's body around the barrel with one knee, the back with her outside knee.

Reins.

Ella pulled the reins in, and Eight knew what came next. She turned at the barrel so steeply that Ella felt her knee bump it.

Ella focused on each of Eight's hooves clawing the dirt, grabbing traction, pushing off again; through Eight's reins, the corners of her sensitive mouth directly connected to Ella's hands.

Then they were clear of the first barrel and headed like a freight train toward the second.

Ella's feet moved automatically, pressing Eight's body around the barrel, harnessing their momentum. As they hurtled around the second barrel, Ella forgot where Eight's body started and hers ended. They took the turn together like a single creature: Eight's hooves were Ella's hooves. Ella's hands were Eight's.

Together they cleared the second barrel, and thundered on to the third.

This was the toughest turn. She had to go around the barrel almost a full revolution, and Eight had sprung off the second barrel with so much momentum that they were coming in too fast.

Ella panicked. If they overshot, they'd lose entire seconds.

She slowed down Eight as they approached the barrel. But they were going too slow now, Ella realized. Still, she'd rather her turn be careful and safe than end in disaster.

Eight was ready when the turn came.

Her whole body tilted into the barrel. Ella had to push her foot back and out of the way to avoid hitting the barrel with her stirrup. Knocking over a barrel would ruin their time.

The turn was long. Ella felt the seconds tick by until Eight had gone all 360 degrees around the barrel, and now faced toward home. It was time to put the pedal to the metal.

Ella crouched as far forward in the saddle as she could, gave Eight plenty of slack in the reins, and said, "Go!"

Eight put on a last burst of speed. Her breath came in huge gulps, in time with the beating of her hooves in the dirt.

The wind pummeled Ella's cheeks. It tossed Eight's mane into her face. But none of that mattered as Eight's powerful muscles tore up the dirt, and her huge, strong legs carried them flying toward the finish line.

They passed through the laser and the buzzer went off. The crowd, as she had hoped, roared.

"Twenty-one point four seconds!" came the announcer's voice, fueling the audience's furor. "Twenty-one point four seconds for the new competitor from Quartz Creek Ranch, and a new best time in today's competition!"

Ella sucked down air as Eight, lathered in sweat, trotted out of the arena. Paul was waiting, and he grabbed Eight by the reins while Mr. Bridle helped Ella out of her saddle. So much adrenaline raced through her that she felt like she was floating, and when Mr. Bridle set her down, she wavered a little on her own two feet.

"That was incredible!" said Paul.

"A really solid run," agreed Ma Etty.

"You did great," said someone behind Ella.

Ella spun at the sound of Jordan's voice. Jordan held Eight by the reins, patting the panting horse's velvety nose. "You should take her for a cool-down walk," Jordan said, handing the reins to Ella.

Ella stared at Jordan, then down at the offering in her hand. Ella was still in shock from the race.

"Yeah, okay," she managed at last, taking the reins.

Why was Jordan here now, after ignoring her all week? But Ella felt too elated by what she'd just done to care.

She'd done it. She'd really done it. And she was at the top of the leaderboard. That belt buckle was practically hers. And the cheering! It had been everything she'd hoped for.

But Ella wanted to see her competition, to be

there when she got that first-place ribbon. So she loosened Eight's saddle cinch and led her around the perimeter of the audience, as Jordan suggested, to cool her down.

Jordan walked with her, not speaking. Ella couldn't read her face, nor the set of her shoulders. But Ella had raced! Her entire body was warm with victory. She and Eight had done it together.

Out in the arena, it was the last competitor's turn.

The tall girl was on fire. Her small spotted horse easily folded its compact body around the turns at breakneck speed. It seemed like she was done as soon as she'd started.

But surely Ella and Eight had gone faster. Except for that slight speed loss before the third barrel . . .

"Twenty point nine seconds!" shouted the announcer. "Holy cow, a twenty-second run at the junior level? With that time, Delia Perez takes the top spot on the leaderboard!"

The crowd went wild. Ella clenched Eight's reins. There went everything.

"Ella?" asked Jordan. "Are you crying?"

Ella stuffed her palms into her eyes, trying to stem the flow of tears, and dropped Eight's reins in the process. "No."

"Why are you crying?" Jordan stared at her, dumbfounded, as she picked up Eight's reins. The announcer was listing rankings.

"Third goes to Mike Rogers," the speaker boomed. "Second, to Ella Pierson!"

"You got second!" Jordan whispered, leaning in. "Second, dude!"

"Don't 'dude' me," Ella said, fresh tears sliding down her face. "I didn't win."

"Seriously?" asked Jordan. "You're crying because you got second instead of first?"

It did sound ridiculous when Jordan put it like that. But Jordan didn't understand what first place meant to Ella.

"I wanted to show you," Ella said. Eight pawed the ground at the distress in her voice. "I wanted to—" She shook her head. "Whatever. It's pointless." And Ella started to walk away, taking Figure Eight with her.

"Wait," said Jordan. "You wanted to show me what?"

"What do you care?" asked Ella, but she didn't have the energy to put any venom behind it. She was tired and sad and she wanted to be alone. "You ditched me."

Jordan met Ella's gaze for a moment, then she flushed and dropped it again, hunching her shoulders. "Yeah. Sorry about that."

That was all she had to say? But the fury Ella expected didn't come. She had been the one who failed Jordan, after all, just like the other girl had predicted.

Second place.

"I just . . ." Jordan bit her lip. "I got so attached to the two of you. To your success. I wanted so badly to help you win."

At this, Ella's mind went blank.

"What?" When she'd had a moment to think, she added, "Then it especially doesn't make sense why you abandoned me right at the end."

"I know!" Jordan was crying now, too, and tried as hard as Ella had to hide it. "But when you asked me about failing and I realized what I'd taken on by teaching you alone, I couldn't take it. It was too much pressure, Ella! Whether you won or lost would be a direct reflection of how good a job I'd done as a teacher. And because I don't have a clue what I'm doing, I didn't want to be the one to make you lose."

"First place," boomed the announcer, "and this handmade belt buckle, go to Delia Perez!"

Ella tried to understand what Jordan was telling

her. "That's . . ." She wanted to say *That's ridiculous,* but that wouldn't help. Ella sighed. "Well, I wish you hadn't left me. I needed you."

"I know," said Jordan miserably. "I'm sorry."

"I am, too." Ella glared at the announcer's box, like the second-place win was actually his fault. "I had meant to get first place. I wanted to win that belt buckle and show you what a great teacher you were."

"Why did you need first place for that?" asked Jordan. "You got second! In an event you only learned a few weeks ago. It's . . ." She searched for the right words. "It's amazing."

"The only reason I'm even here is because you trained me," said Ella. "But maybe you were right. I only got second."

"Only!" A small laugh burst out of Jordan, unexpected, through the tears. "Nothing's ever good enough for you, is it?"

"What about you?" said Ella, sniffling. "Even if I had gotten first place, you wouldn't have believed me. You would have called it a fluke, or—"

"You have natural talent, Ella."

Ella pointed a finger at Jordan. "See? That's exactly what I knew you'd say. I don't, Jordan. You saw me when I first got to Quartz Creek Ranch. Eight was way too much for me. I couldn't jog barrels, not to mention run them. I was a mess."

"You practiced."

"Only what you told me to practice."

Ella knew she wasn't getting anywhere, so before they could argue again, she said, "Whatever, Jordan. You're right. Second place isn't bad. And you helped me get it. I'm not a failure, and neither are you."

With that, she turned and led Figure Eight back to the Quartz Creek Ranch trailer that was parked on the other side of the arena. As she led Eight over, Paul came out and took Eight's reins.

"Go over there! They're giving out the ribbons."

Madison found her as she was walking back to the event area.

"Did Jordan find you? She was looking for you."

Ella just nodded.

Back at the main gate, the attendant was handing out ribbons and trophies. Ella got a huge red ribbon with *2nd* written across it, and a little gold plaque with the show's name.

CHAPTER TWENTY

On the final day of camp, the kids packed their things, and then it was time for one last riding lesson before they boarded the van for the airport.

"Why is this with my stuff?" Jordan held up the big ribbon that Ella had shoved into her duffel bag.

"I put it there." Ella didn't wait to hear Jordan's objection. She headed out to the barn to tack up Eight for the morning lesson. Figure Eight had been in great spirits since the show, and was eager and waiting to run when Ella took her out each morning, anticipating a day of practicing barrels.

But Ella had stopped practicing. Who knew when she'd get a chance to race again? She wanted her free time to play games with the other kids while they still had time, and to give Figure Eight treats.

When the kids showed up with their horses for lessons, Paul was waiting for them in the arena.

"Wanted to do something special for your last day on the ranch," he told them. "Thought I'd give you a tour of what I do around here."

Ash and Drew were almost electric in their saddles.

"Do you have to rope cows?" Drew asked.

"Yep," said Paul, patting the rope hanging from his saddle horn. "To deliver meds, or fix 'em up when they hurt themselves."

"What about calves?"

"Sure, when it's time to brand 'em."

They headed up north across the ranch lands. Paul talked to them about the cattle business and showed off the training a few of his ranch hands were doing with the dogs. Soon Paul fell behind, engaged in conversation with Drew about cattle work. The group approached a fence, the gate closed and latched.

"Can someone get that?" Paul called. Madison was a few horses back, with Ella, Kim, and Jordan at the front.

"I can," said Madison, working her way up.

But Ella was already walking Eight over to the

gate, using her heels to sidle up to the latch. She pulled the lever, let the gate swing open, and allowed the other horses to pass through.

Jordan stared at her, and waited next to her as the caravan passed.

"Nice work," Paul said to Ella as he passed.

"Go on," Ella told Jordan. "So I can close it."

Jordan opened her mouth to say something, then snapped it shut, nodded, and went through. Snatching up the end of the gate, Ella pulled it closed behind Eight and dropped the latch back into place.

As they continued their ride, Ella fell to the back of the line. Jordan, up ahead, slowed down Loco Roco so she fell into step beside her. Ella had a sense of déjà vu.

"When did you learn how to do that?" asked Jordan. "You handled it like a pro."

"I learned when you taught me."

The words hung thickly between them. After a long while, Jordan said, "I actually did something good here." She stared off into the distance as she said it, so Ella wasn't sure if she was talking to herself or to Ella. "I actually helped someone."

"Of course you did."

Jordan shook her head. "But you didn't back down, either. Every time you messed up, you just tried again."

"And again, and again, until it worked. Perseverance is my superpower."

"Or stubbornness," Jordan said, laughing.

\\\

That evening, while the other kids ate churros and played cards at the dining room table, Ella snuck out. She walked to the dark barn, slipping through the creaky door and flipping on the light.

Stopping in front of Figure Eight's stall, Ella grabbed a handful of biscuits. Inside, she saw a familiar scene—the stall appeared empty.

"C'mon now," Ella said. "Get up, silly girl, or there's no treat!"

Hearing this, Figure Eight scrambled up to her feet, just like that first day, and poked her nose through the stall door. Ella opened it and stepped inside, giving Eight the promised reward.

While Eight chewed, Ella combed her fingers through the paint horse's beautiful, splotchy mane. Man. She had gotten so lucky, being assigned to

Figure Eight. Fast, smart, gorgeous—she was as perfect a horse as you could hope to get.

"Thank you," Ella said, leaning her head against Eight's soft, doe-brown neck. Eight stopped chewing and turned her head just a little so she could see Ella's face. "Thank you for putting up with me. For working so hard. For everything."

Eight let out a little nicker, like it had been no big deal for her. Ella had to laugh. Then the horse dipped her head, snuffling the ground nervously.

"Don't worry," said Ella. "Someone else will come along and want to run just as badly as you do." She ran her hand down Eight's forehead, and Eight seemed content with this answer.

It wasn't until Jordan came looking for her that Ella finally gave Eight the rest of the biscuits, and left the barn for the last time.

\\\

Ella and Jordan were on the same flight back to California. They called to each other over the seats until the woman sitting next to Ella insisted Jordan switch places with her. They drew pictures of Figure Eight and Loco Roco for Jordan to show to her siblings.

"Hey," said Jordan suddenly, as the plane started to descend. She tore a piece of paper out of her notebook and handed it to Ella. "My number. Since I don't live so far away . . ."

A grin took over Ella's face. "Yes! I would love to come visit you. I'm sure I can get my dad to drive me out there. Could we ride Mrs. Rose's horses?"

"I'm sure we can," said Jordan. "And I can keep teaching you barrels, if you want." She blushed at that. "And you can meet Antonio!"

That was all Ella needed to hear. If Jordan loved Antonio even a fraction of how much Ella loved Figure Eight, he was sure to be an amazing horse.

"I would love to meet him," Ella said.

"Maybe we can enter more shows," added Jordan, boldly.

Ella's eyes grew wide and eager. "More competitions?" She clapped her hands together. "Definitely yes!"

Jordan burst out laughing. "It's a deal, then."

At the airport, five small Jordan look-alikes and one tall one were waiting outside security. The kids swarmed their older sister the second they saw her, shouting, "Jordy! Jordy!" The tall boy, who must have been her brother Olly, stood off to one side as he waited for the youngsters to finish. Then he swooped in to welcome his sister home, picking her up as he hugged her. Ella rather liked looking at Olly, and definitely wouldn't mind driving out to Clearlake if he was there.

Then Ella recognized Jordan's mom as she stooped down to hug her daughter. What a big, loving family. Her face was lined with kindness; Ella liked her already.

Ella glanced around the waiting area, looking for her own dad. Then she remembered that he had said he was getting off work late, and would meet her outside.

As usual.

After she picked up her luggage and the McAdam family said good-bye, Ella went out the double doors to wait with her luggage. Eventually the BMW pulled up. Dad was on the phone when she climbed in, arguing with someone about contracts and signatures. He gave her a quick hug and tossed her bag into the trunk, and then they were off.

When he got off the phone, he asked, "How was camp?"

"Great," Ella said. "I got second place in a barrel race."

"Only second place?"

She showed him the plaque. "Yeah, Dad. Only second place."

"Well, good job."

"Hey, Dad?"

"Yeah?"

"Can I use your phone?"

"What for?"

"I want to call Mom and tell her."

Her dad took his eyes off the road long enough to turn his head and quirk one eyebrow.

"Your mom?" He handed her the phone and shrugged. "Be my guest."

She found the number quickly and dialed. It rang three times before her mom answered.

"What is it, Greg?" her mom asked brusquely as she answered.

"Hi, Mom."

"Oh, Ella! Honey! Hello!" Her mom exhaled a great sigh, and her voice softened. "So nice to hear from you. How was horse camp?"

"You knew?"

"Your dad told me."

"I won second place in the barrel race."

"Wow!" Mom laughed. "Amazing. You learned to barrel race in the short time you were there?"

"Yep. I had a good teacher."

"Ha. I bet you did. You're a good learner, something any teacher can appreciate. Congratulations, sweetie. I'm so glad you had a good time."

"I made a new friend, too."

"Did you?"

"I think you'd like her."

"I bet I would."

"Can I come visit you, Mom?"

There was a long pause on the other end of the line.

"I thought you weren't interested in visiting, Ella."

"I am now."

Her mom didn't answer for a while, as if perhaps expecting Ella to explain herself. She used to hate those pregnant silences. She never understood what Mom was waiting for.

"Mom," she repeated. "Can I?" She'd explain when she got there.

"Absolutely," her mom said, sounding like she'd been holding her breath. "Have your dad get you a ticket as soon as you get home, before summer break is over."

"Thanks, Mom."

"I can't wait," her mom said. "I love you."

"Love you too," said Ella, for the first time in who knew how long, and hung up the phone.

"Dad?" said Ella.

"Yeah, honey?"

"I need a ticket to go see Mom."

He gave her a sideways look as if he were saying, sarcastically, *So I gathered while I sat here listening.*

"Sure," he said. "Whenever you want."

They went quiet.

After a while, Ella said, "Dad?"

"Yep?"

"Can you drive me out to Clearlake next week? You can, y'know, watch me ride horses. I'm pretty good."

"I bet you are, Miss Prize Winner." He nodded, glancing at Ella and smiling. "Okay. Horseback riding in Clearlake, next Saturday. I'll block off the whole day. Will you put it in my calendar for me, Ell, sweetie?"

ABOUT THE AUTHORS

KIERSI BURKHART grew up riding horses on the Colorado Front Range. At sixteen, she attended Lewis & Clark College in Portland and spent her young adult years in beautiful Oregon—until she discovered her sense of adventure was calling her elsewhere. Now she travels around with her best friend, a mutt named Baby, writing fiction for children of all ages.

AMBER J. KEYSER is happiest when she is in the wilderness with her family. Lucky for her, the rivers and forests of Central Oregon let her paddle, hike, ski, and ride horses right outside her front door. When she isn't adventuring, Amber writes fiction and nonfiction for young readers and goes running with her dog, Gilda.

ACKNOWLEDGMENTS

Big thanks to our agent, Fiona Kenshole, for all the encouragement in the development of this novel; our editor Anna and the rest of the Darby Creek team; and huge thanks to Audra, the best horse teacher there is. Thank you for dropping everything to make sure we did this right, and for teaching Kiersi how to whisper. She needed it.

When she was Ella's age, Kiersi rode another horse that loved to run: an appaloosa pony named Frosty. Together, they took home many first, second, and third place ribbons in the barrel race. Thank you, Frosty, for being the calm in the storm.